I0654129

A Killer, Revisited

By Sheri Chapman

Edited by Eric Myers
Cover by Veronique Poirier

This book is a work of fiction. Names, characters, places and incidents are products of the author's imagination and are not to be construed as real. Any resemblance to actual events, locales, organizations, or persons living or dead, is entirely coincidental.

COPYRIGHT

Copyright © 2020 by Trient Press

All rights reserved. No part of this publication may be reproduced, distributed, or transmitted in any form or by any means, including photocopying, recording, or other electronic or mechanical methods, without the prior written permission of the publisher, except in the case of brief quotations embodied in critical reviews and certain other noncommercial uses permitted by copyright law. For permission requests, write to the publisher, addressed "Attention: Permissions Coordinator," at the address below.

Criminal copyright infringement, including infringement without monetary gain, is investigated by the FBI and is punishable by up to five years in federal prison and a fine of $250,000.

Except for the original story material written by the author, all songs, song titles, and lyrics mentioned in the novel Secret of the Sword are the exclusive property of the respective artists, songwriters, and copyright holders

Trient Press
3375 S Rainbow Blvd
#81710, SMB 13135
Las Vegas,NV 89180

Ordering Information:
Quantity sales. Special discounts are available on quantity
purchases by corporations, associations, and others. For details,
contact the publisher at the address above.
Orders by U.S. trade bookstores and wholesalers. Please contact Trient
Press: Tel: (775) 996-3844; or visit www.trientpress.com.

Printed in the United States of America

Publisher's Cataloging-in-Publication data
Chapman, Sheri
A title of a book : A Killer, Revisited
ISBN
   Paperback 978-1-953975-11-9
   E-book   978-1-953975-12-6

Dedications:

This story is dedicated to all who believe in me. I especially want to thank my family, friends, and fans for your continued support.

My teacher colleagues, David Lynn and Theresa Walls, honored me with praise, and I feel humbled. I also want to thank my beta readers and friends, Laura Kilburn, and Alaya Gunnell-Brake. I appreciate their thoughts and opinions. I thank my father, Leo Mohrbacher, for his years and dedication to the Air Force, and my bowling alley veteran friends, David Parker and Matt Kilburn, helped me brainstorm military ideas. Josh Wade, a wonderful young man, thank you so much for helping me with gun, knife, and Electro rounds ideas. I thank my mother, Jean Anderson, who is always supportive in any way I need her to be. I love her insights. I want to thank my daughter, Emily Branson, for help on the character, Sylvia Turner's research focus, and my daughter, Mikaela Branson, for taking an idea I have and offering great suggestions. Lastly, a special thank you goes to my editor, Eric Myers, for helping me to become better than I was. His insights and advice have reformed my writing, and I am deeply appreciative.

Thank you to all for your love and support. You keep my passion alive.

Books by Sheri Chapman -
Published by Trient Press

Wild Passion *(Book 1 of the Passion series – historical romance)*

Passions of the Heart *(Book 2 of the Passion series – historical romance)*

"Chief Spirit Bear: Rise to Power" *– (A Passion Series novella)*

"Eyes with No Soul*" (YA paranormal suspense)*

A Killer, Revisited *– (futuristic detective suspense)*

Website:
https://prayerpawpuppies.wixsite.com/authorsherichapman/books

PRESENT DAY: A Man on a Mission

Wylie's home office was tiny with no windows. Its single light flickered, and the effect excited him. The man rummaged through an arsenal in a large canvas bag in the closet.

Wylie slid black gloves over his work-hardened hands and clenched a few times.   Next, he examined a heavy Bowie knife. It caught the light as he turned it. He practiced a few stabbing motions.

Satisfied, the assassin removed his gloves and placed both items carefully in a smaller, traveling duffel with the rest of his dark, plain clothing.

This was the night. Wylie, The Chameleon, was exhilarated. This was not an assignment and he a mere pawn. This was a mission of his own. The excitement of obtaining his freedom motivated him. However, he knew he must maintain an air of normalcy around his handlers.

Wylie straightened, relaxed his shoulders, and controlled his breath.

If things went well, he was on his way to true freedom.

PRESENT DAY: Sylvia Turner

Sylvia Turner worked on her master's thesis. Hours without a break, she stood and accidentally bumped one of the piles on her desk. An article fluttered to the floor. She sighed and grabbed the paper, not caring if she rumpled it.

Immediately contrite, Sylvia smoothed the wrinkles from the work and replaced it on the pile. She patted it gently then ran her fingers through her hair.

The young blonde stared at her accumulation of research on how the fragmentation of habitat affects the spread of prion diseases, ultimately resulting in one-hundred percent fatality rates among cervids, or deer population, across the Midwest.

Sylvia's phone charged on her desk. She'd depleted the battery after a morning of questioning upper-level conservation officers who were of little help.

She paced, glanced at her desk and phone, then paced more quickly. She felt her frustration level rising to explosive levels. She had little data to support anything conclusive.

"I need a break."

In the bathroom, she looked at her reflection. On a whim, Sylvia pulled her long waves back into a honey-colored ponytail and put on her running suit.

Her phone rang. She hurried to the device and glanced at caller ID. She reached for the phone then paused.

"I'll call them back when I return," she mumbled, "I need a few miles of freedom to clear my mind."

Evening began to settle on the land. There was just enough light for a few miles of liberty. Sylvia chewed gum as she placed the front door key under the potted plant with the purple base.

The slap of her feet on the pavement felt as relaxing as a massage. With each step, Sylvia felt the tension flowing from her body. Deep breaths rejuvenated her brain and rekindled her determination to accomplish her goals.

For now, just for now, she was determined to let her mind wander.

As she ran, she pondered the fabled "runner's high". It wasn't something she believed in, necessarily, but she had to admit that she did have a sense of release she didn't get with other types of exercise. She felt unrestricted, like she could accomplish anything. Though in no way she considered herself high.

Maybe it's the term 'high' I have problems with.

Finally, she turned for home.

When Sylvia approached the front door, a shadow flitted across her face. She unlocked the door and shuddered as goose bumps rose on her arms. She hesitated a moment before pushing the door open.

"You're being silly," she chided herself softly.

She rented in this neighborhood because it was safe. She would spend nights alone, she knew, and was okay with it. For a moment, she thought about inviting her father over for dinner, but quickly rejected the idea.

Most of the time, she plotted ways to escape talking about his... projects. His ideas were scientifically based, of course, but were truly "out there."

TWO YEARS AGO: Sylvia Turner's house

A knock resounded through her house. Sylvia sat at her desk with stacks of research around her. She hopped up and slapped a hand on a stack of papers to keep them from toppling. She peeked out the hole and her jaw clenched. It was her father. She opened the door anyway.

"Hello, Sylvia."

"Hi, Dad," she sighed. "Come on in."

Mathew Turner entered with several files tucked under his arm.

"What do you have this time?" she asked. Her hand propped on a hip.

Her father sat on her couch, slightly out of breath. His eyes were vibrant and flashed with excitement.

"Just hear me out, Sylvia. I know your passion is environmental biology, but that's not where the money is."

"Dad, we've talked about this a million times. You do you, and I'll do me."

"I have a great opportunity for you, Dear."

"I don't care, Dad. What you do is unethical. It was kind of okay when people volunteered for your... experiments, but now you're at the prison... what you do isn't right."

Dr. Turner's lips pursed. "Just hear me out."

Sylvia settled on the chair and leaned back. Another soft sigh. "Make it quick. I have work to do." Her eyes flitted to the piles on her desk.

"Sylvia. I love you. You're the only person of meaning in my life. I hate to see you whittle your life away... studying deer or something silly like that. I know you think what I do is unethical, but if you work with me, you'll see how it's the key to the future. I want to share that ride with you."

"Dad. Do people want to participate in your studies? Have you even asked them?"

"That's beside the point."

"No. It isn't. Even prisoners... have rights."

"Hum. Well, we may not see eye-to-eye on every point, but the bigger picture is how we can create a better future." Her father's eyes flashed.

"By sacrificing inmates?" she scoffed. "Better future or not. Your ways are unethical. No future can justify that."

"If you want to study the deer population, you go where the deer are. You try to figure out what's killing them, what food benefits them, and so on. I'm doing the same. I'm studying a population of men who are incarcerated. It's easier to collect data when your subjects are confined to a certain area."

"That's hardly the same, Dad."

"You're right about that. No one cares about the deer population... or wolf... or bird, not really. People will care about what I do, once I'm published. Please, Sylvia. Please, come along with me."

Sylvia intentionally sighed louder. "Dad, I love you, too, but I'm truly tired of talking about this. How 'bout I make us breakfast-for-dinner? I'm going to prove my work is just as important before this is all over with. But first let's eat. No more talk about the future, okay?"

"You bet, Honey. But this isn't over."

Sylvia nodded. "You can turn on the television if you want." She headed for the kitchen.

Dr. Turner flipped on the TV. When his daughter was out of sight, he went to the secret fireproof safe in her closet. He slid a few files inside and put a few winter coats on top. Tomorrow, when she had class, he'd return and move the safe to a more secluded location in her house.

PRESENT DAY: Wylie and Sylvia meet

It was too easy, really. Wylie took the key from its hiding spot, unlocked the door, and simply walked inside. He melded into the shadows to wait. His fingers twitched on the knife handle.

The ability to camouflage in full sight was a skill that earned him the nickname, The Chameleon. He willed it, and stealth mode activated. Wylie didn't understand the technology, only that it certainly worked. His designers made the perfect killer. They thought of everything. Everything except the ability to control him. He grinned in the dark. He didn't mind carrying out their assignments. But he loved the ones he initiated on his own.

Wylie watched the slender young woman hesitate in her entryway. She shuddered and mumbled something before stepping into her house.

<><><><><>

Sylvia took a quick shower then started a pot of coffee. She glanced at her desk, piled high with unfinished work and yawned.

The young scientist wasn't a fan but poured a cup. She added sugar and cream to soften the bite. Tentatively, Sylvia took a sip then added more sugar before settling down to begin another long night

None interviewed, thus far, were able to answer her many questions about CWD. Until she got answers, sleep would not come easy. She stretched and took another sip.

With a sigh, she hammered away again at her keyboard. Answers to her inquiries weren't going to be found in journal articles. She needed to locate and interview more professionals in the conservation field. Maybe, just maybe, she would be the first person with a breakthrough.

It was important she showed her father her research was just as important, but she'd do things the right way, *the moral way*.

After compiling a list, Sylvia checked her missed calls. A slow smile brightened her face. With glee, she punched the redial button.

Out of the corner of her eye, she saw the shrouded figure approach. Sylvia screamed and sprang from her seat as the phone fell from her hand.

"Hello, Sylvia," Wylie said. "A moment of your time?" He laughed, "It's all you have."

"Wh - who are you?" she stammered. She moved her desk chair between them.

"Funny you should ask," Wylie rasped. "How well are you acquainted with your father's work?"

What?"

"Think. I'll give you time to process."

A few moments later, "Umm… a little. I keep my distance from his research. I don't care for his… methodologies."

"Ah," Wylie said. "In that case, all I really need are the papers."

Sylvia's eyes widened. Her fingers tightened on the chair. "What are you talking about?"

"His case notes from his work at the prison. Where are they?" He took a menacing step toward her.

Sylvia backed a few steps. "I - I don't know. Why don't you ask him? Why did you come here and not just call?"

Wylie took another step into the light. The Bowie knife grabbed her attention. He smiled as he advanced.

"Why are you doing this?" she whispered. Then, louder, "If I had his papers, I'd tell you."
The Chameleon's eyes glittered, and he raised the knife. His wicked smile sent a shiver down her spine. Sylvia pushed the chair as hard as she could and ran. Her screams filled the air along with the husky laughter of her executioner.

PRESENT DAY: Police Precinct

Edmond, Oklahoma, pop. 81,500. Its crime rate was low for a city of its size, murders still occurred, though never serial murder cases.

Jewels Polten worked hard to be the leading homicide detective for Edmund City PD. Her phone rang. After a brief conversation, she summoned her partner, Joe Combs.

"Joe, we've got something." she said excitedly.

"What is it, Jewels?" asked the bald, middle-aged man. He looked down from his lofty 6'4" to the slender brunette seated at her marred desk.

"The Oklahoma Department of Wildlife Conservation just called. One of their high-ranking officials got a message on his phone that's concerning."

Joe scratched his head. "Why are they calling us? Isn't this out of our jurisdiction?"

"They want us to listen to the message. It's from a University of Central Oklahoma student contacting them for her research. They think something happened to her. If so, that would be our jurisdiction."

Joe nodded. "Okay."

"The girl left her name and number with several people. They tried her phone and no response. They want us to check it out."

"Let's listen to this message first. Then we'll get an address."

The message was indeed disturbing. The beginning was a piercing scream. Next, indistinguishable feminine and masculine voices interacted for a few minutes. Then endless horrific screams along with the sounds of a violent struggle.

One could imagine bodies being forcefully thrown onto furniture that cracked then crashed to the floor. The most horrific sound of all, though, was the sound of gurgling and scratching followed by complete silence.

"Let's get a copy of this to forensics," Jewels said. "Maybe they can clear up the voices on the audio."

Joe said, "On it."

PRESENT DAY: Wylie

The phone rang in Wylie's office. It was the lab, again.

"Hello?" he answered.

"Wylie, your tracker came out again. You need to get to the lab," the tech demanded.

"Hey, don't I always respond to your summons?" His words were clipped.

"Yes." He hesitated, "But that's not the point."

"I don't want a damn tracker. That's the point."

The technician continued, "Sorry, Wylie. It's part of your... agreement."

"An agreement indicates both sides approve," he growled.

"Your situation is... complicated. You're the first of your kind. We need to know where you are..."

"No, I don't think you do." Wylie slammed the phone. This puppet-on-a-string act was getting old, fast.

The phone immediately rang again.

ONE YEAR AGO: Secret Army lab

Dr. Bellamy James just completed another perfect clone. He stepped back to admire the new soldier, 183 cm, muscular, with advanced military training implanted in his brain. It sat at an exam table in an exercise room.

The preeminent Dr. James's experiments were conducted in complete security. One would literally have to fight through an army to get to the lab.

"Okay, Sam." Bellamy's lab assistant stood next to the clone with a highly advanced remote-control device ready. "Let's start with sequence One."

"Got it, Doctor." Sam pushed a few buttons on the small hand-held device and then made some comparative observations. "Leads are good. Signal active across all nodes."

"Excellent," Dr. James said with a big grin. "Let's start at level five this time. Activate."

"Beginning activation." Sam looked at the small control device and punched in a sequence.

The clone headed to a treadmill. Sam avidly watched with bright eyes. He pushed a few more buttons and turned a dial on the device. "Level five Sequence One. In three, two, one."

The soldier immediately ran with intensity. His legs were a blur as they pounded on the spinning track.

"Level five, Doctor." Sam said as he read the data collected from the treadmill, "Twenty-two miles per hour. Pulse 82, Reps 16. No indication of muscle fatigue."

"Nice. Very nice," Dr. James said. "Okay, level seven. No, let's go full on. Level ten."

Sam smiled and said, "Sure thing." His hand moved to the dial on the remote and twisted.

Bellamy smiled at his assistant's excitement. This was their first time at level ten. He had to confess: he was excited, too.

"Sequence One at Level Ten in three, two, one."

The whirl of the treadmill and the hammering of the clone's feet were now loud enough to require raised voices. The soldier's arms and legs were a vibrating blur.

"This is really cool, Doc," Sam said. His eyes were aglow with excitement. "Pulse 94, Resp 20. Thirty-five miles per hour. I think he can give a little more. Man, we should put him in the Olympics."

"That is beneath him," Dr. James said. "That would be like entering a Rembrandt in a county fair."

They watched the soldier run without a misstep for another five minutes.

"No dip in body readings, sir," Sam said. "But his speed is now forty." A huge grin split his face.

"Let's call it a day," Dr James said with a light slap to Sam's shoulder. "I would definitely say he's fit for duty."

"Well. Physically anyway," Sam said. "He's still just a meat puppet."

Sam noticed Bellamy's lowered brows.

"What did I tell you about using that term?"

Sam shrugged apologetically. "Sorry, Doc. But he still has no soul. No personality. He only works when we use this remote." Sam lifted the object with its mention. "Makes him just an expensive marionette."

Bellamy sighed. "Yeah, I know. I almost have the solution for that. Come with me."

The doctor dragged his assistant into an enormous, locked chamber filled with humans in varying stages of development. Some embryonic, some adolescent, and some were fully developed muscular specimens. They were unconscious. The younger versions were in huge tubes filled with a thick liquid. The fully developed specimens were in pods and monitored by rows of equipment.

"Sir?" Sam asked in shocked wonder. His feet rooted where he stood. He could barely do more than stare.

Dr. James chuckled.

"What... what are they doing here?" Sam asked. His eyes wide as he studied the many figures. "There're... so many."

Dr. James chose his words. "Do you remember Hitler's philosophy about the perfect soldier?"

"Yes. He experimented on babies. He believed if parents withheld nurturing, the children wouldn't develop empathy. Hitler wanted the perfect assassin, and he believed this was the way to create cold-blooded killers. But," reminded the aide, "the babies failed to thrive and withered away. They died without human touch."

"Precisely," said Dr. James with a smile. His eyes gleamed and his chest puffed a bit.

Sam laughed. "That's one way to bypass raising a kid... without human touch."

Dr. James's laugh joined Sam's. "Yeah, I guess so. Clones aren't used to human touch, so I've done what Hitler couldn't. I've created an uncaring, disconnected soldier." He corrected himself. "*Soldiers.* I am the first scientist of my kind. Mark my words, young man. Many will follow my work."

"Sir? No offense, but they don't really look up to fighting. What I see is a collection of meat puppets." Sam scratched his head. "Are you saying we'll have to test all of these... specimens? Like we're doing with Unit One?" Sam, in shocked amazement, circled slowly with his arms out wide, staring at them all. "How, sir? We don't have the time."

"Activation is the next phase. When these Rangers are ready, these dormant soldiers will become something you will only see in your wildest dreams – once another doctor and I prove our hypothesis."

"What?" Sam muttered with widened eyes.

Dr. James declared, "They will become human."

"Sir?"

"They will function on their own. To use your term, they *will* have souls."

Sam stared open-mouthed.

PRESENT DAY: Detectives Jewels and Joe

"Scenes like that make me want to get out of this line of work," Jewels said. Her shoulders drooped as she massaged her lower back. Her hair was more than a little disheveled.

"That was the worst crime scene I ever saw," said Joe, taking off his latex gloves. He dropped them into a bag on his way out. "It was worse than the two priors."

Jewels nodded. "Now I know why the media dubbed him as the 'Eat Your Heart Out Killer'. I agree, it was worse than the other two. He's escalating. I'd hate to be the guys bagging the body. Or what's left of it. Those are the ones who need a new line of work." said Jewels. "It'll take them all day to find the pieces. God, I'm so tired I can't think anymore."

Joe looked at her. His brows furrowed a bit.

"This is bad timing, I know. You feel like grabbing a bite before heading home?"

Jewels looked at Joe and noticed the dark shadows under his slightly blood-shot eyes.

"God help me, but yes on both." Jewels said with a little sigh. "But I want to go to the precinct to get cleaned up first."

Joe nodded. "I know what you mean."

"We have a real sick-o in our city," said Jewels.

PRESENT DAY: Wylie

Wylie noticed a difference in himself. He was beginning to experience more... *what were they? Brain functions?* He was continuing to develop thinking outside the box when compared to the expected-mission-only thinking. He was becoming curious. *Yes, that is the word. Curious.*

As a soldier, he was trained to be alert and attentive to all realms of possible threats. This was more than that, though. He wanted to see who investigated his murders out of *curiosity*.

Immediately upon seeing the petite woman in charge, he was hooked. She was fiery and fearless. She swept in and gave orders. A short while later, though, she reappeared from the house a sickly color. She shuffled stiffly and looked as though she was going to be ill.

A smile curved his lips and put a twinkle in his eye. Her overreaction to his murder scene was amusing. In fact, it made him want to know more about her. With a chuckle, Wylie followed the couple back to the police headquarters.

PRESENT DAY: Detectives Jewels and Joe

Jewels showered at the precinct. She took her time dressing and combing her hair. Finally, she stepped back into the bustle of the station. Joe stood as soon as he saw her. His hair was damp, and his eyes seemed a little brighter.

She answered before the question fell from his lips. "I feel a little better. But not much. The shower helped some. I think I'm going to feel dirty for a while."

"Yes, I'm starting to feel a bit better, too. Come on," he said. "Let's get outta here. I know just the place."

Jewels allowed Joe to gently guide her to his vehicle with a tender hand on her shoulder.

"How about you leave your car here for the night? I'll swing by to get you on my way in."

"I don't know..."

"Let's eat and then you can tell me if you want to go home or come back for your car."

"Fair enough."

Neither spoke during the trip. It was fifteen minutes later when Joe pulled into a small sports grill.

Jewels looked at him with an arched brow.

He said, "A beer will do you good. Hell, maybe watching a game is just what the doctor ordered."

Joe held the door open for her.

"Thank you," she mumbled.

"Let's get that corner in the back," Joe said. "We can talk, watch television, and see who's coming in."

"Sure," she said.

Their backs were to the door when it opened and closed of its own accord.

They settled into the table. Jewels pressed her fingers to her temple.

"Headache?" Joe asked quietly.

"Not yet." she sighed, "Just a little pressure behind my eyes."

"You feel up to a beer, then?"

Jewels looked at him. "Sure, why not? If a headache roars to life, it won't be because of a beer."

"Okay, okay." he said. Joe held up his hands in surrender, and she gave a soft smile.

Finally, their server came. "Do you know what you want yet, or do you need a few more minutes?"

"Bacon cheeseburger, medium, with fries." Joe said.

"May I have the chicken strip basket?" Jewels asked. She smiled and looked at Joe. "I'm not quite ready for red meat."

"Sure," the server said. She scribbled on her pad of paper.

"Oh," Joe called as she was turning to go, "and bring us a couple of beers, too. Whatever you have on tap."

"And, if you don't mind, water... with lemon," Jewels added.

"I'll be back in sec." she said.

"You sure you're okay?" Joe asked. He lightly drummed his fingers on the table without realizing.

"No," Jewels answered. "What if that... monster stays a while in our town? I wanted Lead Detective, but after today... that scene... makes me wonder."

"Come on, Jewels, you're being unfair to yourself. I don't know of anyone who could handle a scene like that one. You've been Lead for a year now, and you're a damn good one. Don't let that butchery make you doubt yourself."

The server returned with their drinks.

"Thanks, Joe," she said. She lifted her beer and clinked his glass. "I needed that."

"Look at the bright side. At least we don't have to be the guys who deliver that message to the parents," Joe said. "I'd equally hate to be those guys."

Jewels swallowed. "Me, too."

They watched the game on television for a bit. When their food arrived, both took bites.

"I'm hungry, but I don't know how much I can eat," Jewels said after finally swallowing her first bite.

"Try to eat half," Joe advised.

"Yes, dad."

Joe raised a brow. She grinned and picked up her beer, so he picked up his as well.

"Do you want to decompress by talking about anything?" Joe asked.

"Here?"

"No one's close enough to overhear." He shrugged. "Good thing about sport bars. They're loud."

Jewels closed her eyes for a second and nodded. "Well, I'm worried. This is the third strike by this guy, and he's progressing. Each scene is worse than the one prior. My gut tells me we haven't seen the last of our Killer. He's very angry... and *that* bothers me a lot."

"I agree. Tomorrow we'll look further into the vic. Get a handle on who she was."

"Of course."

"I mean, Jewels, we'll do it *tomorrow*... not tonight." he said with a gentle smile.

Jewels chuckled. "Am I that transparent?"

"No. Well..." he winked. "Maybe. I know how you can't shut off that brain of yours. But if you don't eat or sleep, you won't last long."

"Point taken," Jewels said and took another bite of her chicken.

They worked on their meal and watched the game a bit longer.

"You want another beer?" Joe asked.

"Yes, one more. You want the rest of my chicken?" she asked, sliding the basket toward him. "It's good, but I'm done."

"Thanks." Joe pulled the food closer.

"Is Cara around?"

"She's out of town this week. She's got a presentation at Fort Bragg." Joe bit into a strip.

"Nice. She gets to go to the Center of the Universe, huh?"

"She's having a good time. She loves the history of the place. We'll have you over when she gets back."

Jewels took a long pull from her beer. "Where's Kaylee? Did she go with Cara?"

Joe laughed. "She's in her teens. She won't have anything to do with us. She's staying the night with Lola."

Jewels nodded. "I'll look forward to visiting when Cara returns and gets settled. When you're finished, I do think I want my car. I'd feel like I didn't have my gun on a stake out if I left my car."

"I understand. I just wanted to offer in case you didn't feel like driving." Joe pushed the plates away and patted his stomach.

"You chauffeur me around all day, so I need the driving practice. I don't want to lose my edge."

"Women drivers have an edge?" Joe asked with a laugh.

She punched him playfully as they headed out.

PRESENT DAY: Wylie

Wylie stood to the side of the couple at the table in the back. He couldn't help himself; he was fascinated. He'd never been exposed to non-military behavior before, and he felt himself drawn in.

He watched the body language between the two and listened to the conversation. *Is this what caring for another looked like?* Wylie noticed it was vastly different from the strict discipline he knew. Even with all the gifts the Army had blessed him with, *this was the unknown.*

The woman detective. She was a novelty. Were other women so... vibrant? Her glossy dark hair shone in the bar light. She had bright, animated eyes, even through the stress her body displayed.   And her lips. He watched her mouth as she ate, drank, and spoke. They were not painted but were still pink and shiny. Wylie had to stay his hand from reaching out to touch them.

When the duo left, the Chameleon found himself staring at the detective's water glass. He noticed she liked lemon. For some reason, that stuck in his mind.

PRESENT DAY: Dr. Mathew Turner

Dr. Turner relaxed on his imported leather couch and turned on his television.

He crossed his men's black Sorel slippers on his hand-carved sandalwood coffee table and settled back into the cushions.

I'm long overdue for a mindless movie. It may be some time before I have another moment like this.

A loud knock at the door startled him. Mathew took his time to answer. He looked through the elegant glass in the center of his door and saw two uniformed officers.

What could this be about?

He pulled his thin silk robe tighter as he opened the portal.

The red-headed police woman stood closer than her Hispanic male partner.

"Hello, officers."

"Dr. Mathew Turner?" The woman's voice was low and husky.

"Yes."

The man stepped forward. "I'm Officer Rodriguez and this is Officer Walsh," They flashed their badges.

"Would you mind if we came in?" the woman asked.

"What's this about?" Turner tried to read their body language.

Officer Rodriguez said, "We have some bad news. May we talk inside, sir?"

Dr. Turner allowed them into his foyer.

"What's happened?" he asked.

"It's about your daughter," Officer Walsh said.

"You might want to sit, sir," Officer Rodriguez said.

Mathew's knees were suddenly weak. He slumped onto a nearby chair.

"Is Sylvia okay?"

"She was a victim of a violent crime, sir," Walsh said gently.

"Oh, God!" Mathew covered his face with his hands and sobbed. The sounds of his sorrow eventually died down though his shoulders continued to shake as grief tore through his body.

The officers stood quietly, with their hands clasped behind their backs. Walsh handed the doctor a pack of Kleenex.

"We're deeply sorry, Dr. Turner. Is there anything we can do for you?" Rodriguez asked.

Walsh said, "Her death is under investigation by our best detectives."

"Th - thank you," the doctor said.

"Sir, we need to ask this." Rodriguez began.

"You need me to identify the body, don't you?"

"Yes, sir," Rodriguez said.

Welsh leaned forward a little. "If you're prepared, we can take you to her now."

Dr. Turner nodded.

PRESENT DAY: Detectives Jewels and Joe

A few days later, Jewels received a call from the forensics lab.

"This is Detective Polten."

"Yes, Detective, a suspicious letter arrived for you this morning."

"Suspicious? Isn't everything you guys look at suspicious? What, is the letter written in cut out letters or something?"

"Umm, well. As a matter of fact, yes. It's clear. Do you want us to send it up?"

"Yes, please. This outta be interesting."

When it arrived Polten said, "Joe, come take a look at this."

Joe read over her shoulder. "Darkness is nothing... darkness is everything."

Jewels looked up at him.

"I've seen this before," Joe said.

"Okay, some nonsense about darkness." Jewels said, "What do you think this means?"

"Some idiot's been watching too much T.V. He's toying with us."

"He? What makes you think it's a male?" Jewels said. "Wait, do you think our guy sent this?"

"He's telling us he is darkness, and we won't catch him."

"That's bullshit." Jewels stood quickly and knocked her chair to the floor.

Joe looked at her with a raised eyebrow.

"I'm fine," she said and strode to their murder board with three pictures of victims. The words 'science field' were pinned under each one. "We know each vic is in the field of science."

"Yeah, but why scientists?" Joe asked. "And Sylvia Turner was just a student, though. What would he have against her?"

"Not sure. But, if this letter really is from our guy, then maybe science is not the only link."

"Yeah, that's a whole new level of crazy, isn't it? Maybe the victims were just in the wrong place at the wrong time, the science thing is just coincidence?" Joe said. "Or maybe he's got something against scientists and is systematically picking them off? Could this be more political? Scientists are ruining our world or some such thing?"

"I don't think so. These killings seem to be... a little personal."

"It could be that our guy just likes killing." Joe said.

Jewels looked at him. "He obviously enjoys it, I'll give you that, but this guy is angry about something. It is not random. He knows you and I are on the case. That means he is observing the crime scene. He's methodical. And he can get information. It's like you said. He's toying with us. He wants us to know who is calling the shots. This is more than just angry at scientists."

Jewels pinned the letter to the murder board.

"Let's start interviewing." Joe said.

"My thoughts exactly," Jewels said. "Where do you think we should begin? The first victim was Rafael Torrent, cryogenics."

"And victim two was Fritz Muller, German pathologist. Let's start where these scientists work. See where it leads."

Jewels sat at her computer and clacked at the keyboard. She read for a few minutes.

When she looked up, she said, "So tomorrow we'll visit the cryogenics lab, Technology of Tomorrow, and The Disease Center."

"It's as good a place as any."

"What about the Turner girl?" Jewels asked as she stood back up. "What's her story then? She just seems to be the odd one out. She was a scientist, but what could she have done to piss off our guy so much?"

"Hopefully, we'll find out," Joe replied.

"Sometime today, I'd like to see what more you can dig up about her," Jewels said. "Maybe run some checks on all those phone calls she was making."

Joe nodded. "Will do."

THREE YEARS EARLIER: Private practice counseling office

Dr. Mathew Turner was average sized with dark brown hair cut short. He was a psychologist and received his PhD from Stanford and did post grad research in Criminal Counseling. He spent both day and night studying how external factors, such as the child's environment, nutrition, and genetics affected brain and personality development. His name was associated with many published experiments where subjects were paid to participate in his research.

Georgia, Dr. Turner's receptionist, called.

"Hello?" said Dr. Turner.

"Yes, Doctor. There's a man here to see you. He says he has an appointment, but he's not on the books."

"Yes, Georgia. Please show him in," Dr. Turner said.

The blonde receptionist, in her mid-twenties, led a tall man into the office. The visitor was a thick gentleman;

solid. He wore an olive-colored tee that stretched across his muscular girth and a pair of new-looking jeans. The other detail that hinted at a military background were his combat boots.

Dr. Turner noticed the guest's stern expression and how his beady eyes locked on his. The visitor licked his thick lips slowly and waited for the secretary to leave .

Mathew gave his PA a slight smile and a nod. "Thank you, Georgia. That'll be all."

"Yes, Doctor." Georgia threw a curious look at the visitor and stepped out of the office, softly closing the door behind her.

A few moments after her departure, the man finally spoke.

"Hello, Dr. Turner."

"Nice to finally meet you, General Hawkins."
Dr. Turner walked forward to extend his enormous hand.

The general's grip was strong. He turned the doctor's hand until it was underneath his and pumped it twice. Then he let go abruptly.

"Please, I'd rather you not call me by my name." The general's unfriendly gaze continued to study him.

"Oh," Dr. Turner said with surprise. "Okay." He took an unconscious step back.

They stood, awkwardly appraising each other, until finally, the doctor asked, "So, why did you want to meet, if I may ask?"

"I've read your publications," the general said. "You're an expert in developmental psychology."

Mathew nodded and waited for him to continue.

"How would you like to study the brain of a more... deviant population?"

"Go on." Dr. Turner's eyes widened with interest.

"I need a man to work with me on a top-secret project involving inmates and their behavior." The general's expression never changed.

"I'm listening."

"This is a classified military operation. It is imperative no one is to know of its existence. Do you understand?"

"Of course," the doctor said.

"You may not even talk about it if you should decide this project isn't for you," the officer said gruffly.

"Understood, sir."

"You have a background in criminal psychology." It wasn't really a question.

"Yes, sir, but – "

The man interrupted, "How would you like to counsel inmates?"

"Um, well, I – "

"You'll do a few government-requested experiments, as well," the general explained. His thick, dark brows raised.

"Really?" Dr. Turner stopped trying to talk.

"The state penitentiary a few hours away. Your cover is counseling death-row inmates, just lead a few group sessions. Your real purpose is to capture the soul of a man once his life is over."

The doctor's eyes widened. "How did you...?"

"You're just the man I've been looking for," the general said. "Like I said, I read your research. Then I began watching you. You're exactly who I need for this program."

TWO YEARS ELEVEN MONTHS AGO: Private meeting room for prison inmates

While the guards stood outside the door, Dr. Turner entered the small interrogation room. It had barred windows with an additional layer of plexiglass for privacy. The inmate was chained to anchors on the floor. He sat at a small metal table; Mathew across from him. He tried to adjust his chair, but it, too, was secured.

The prisoner was a smaller man, about five foot eight by the doctor's guess, thin but wiry. His size surprised Matt. After reading his file, he expected a more robust man.

"Hello, Wright. I'm Dr. Turner. I'm the death row prison counselor."

"Hi, Doc," he said, looking up. His large blue eyes had a hard edge. "I appreciate the opportunity to get out of my cell and actually hold a conversation, but you're wasting your time with me."

"Most men say that," the doctor said. "I can help more than you think. Give me a chance."

Wright laughed. "Oh, it's nothing against you, Doc. I know me, and I'm not rehabilitatable."

"Humor me, let's explore why you believe that. You want conversation, anyway, so why not?"

"You're not going to write a book or anything, are you?"

Dr. Turner said, "I do run studies and write papers for publication, but no, your story won't be used for plot development."

"Good."

"If I may ask, why?" Dr. Turner rested his clasped hands on the edge of the table.

"My story shouldn't be told," Wright said, leaning back. The chains clattered with his movement.

"But why? What's your reasoning behind that?"

"I'm a killer, Doc." Wright's features were surprised. "I don't want what I do glorified."

"You could go down in history. Like… Dahmer or Manson."

"I don't deserve fame. I'm a caged animal. My body is my prison."

"Interesting, I'd like to hear more about that." Dr. Turner shifted in his uncomfortable prison chair.

"You want my down and dirty? Okay, my first kill was when I was thirteen, but I'm sure you already knew that. My mom's boyfriend just beat the shit out of her, and I was tired of it. A red haze filled my gaze, and before I knew what I was doing, I stabbed him in the back."

"And you kept stabbing."

"Yes. It was exhilarating. His blood on my hands made me feel... rejuvenated and..."

"Powerful." The doc nodded knowingly.

"Yes." Wright sighed. "Like I was reborn... like I was in control."

"But yet you weren't."

Wright scratched a spot above his ear. His sandy hair rippled with the action.

"No. But for the first time in my life, I felt whole. I done what my mom couldn't."

"So that was turning the corner for you," said Dr. Turner.

"Damn straight, Doc. It changed my life, but I'm not proud of how." The inmate stretched.

"So, tell me what motivates you." The doctor watched him closely.

"Well, I'd have to say... mostly..." He leaned forward and placed a thumb under his chin and rested a finger against his cheekbone. He tapped it softly as he contemplated. "Revenge."

"He hurt you and your mom."

"Yes. And killing became how I handled everyone who had betrayed me."

"So, you killed them all?"

"And everyone they cared about," Wright looked down and ran his fingers through his hair.

"Your actions while you talk reveal you have remorse." Turner leaned forward a little.

"Doc, I don't know how to answer that. I know what I do is 'wrong.'" Wright made quotation marks with his fingers. "I can care about people, I think, but if that person ever crosses me, they're dead. I feel bad for losing control, but I don't feel sorry in the sense you mean."

"That makes sense. A true psychopath doesn't have feelings of guilt or remorse." They studied one another. Dr. Turner continued, "You're intelligent and are aware it's considered 'wrong,'" he too made air quotes, "but it's not wrong for you."

"I'd say that's pretty accurate, Doc. I don't like losing control. That's why I feel like a prisoner... whether I'm behind bars or not."

"Very good self-analysis, Wright," Turner said.

"I've had some time to think, Doc."

"I suppose you have," Dr. Turner said. "You know? I didn't think you'd be as receptive to... open up to me so soon."

"When you're all alone for days on end, you welcome any conversation." Wright gave a weak smile.

"I'll bet," he said, looking at his watch, "I'll look forward to working with you a lot, Wright. This was a surprisingly good session, a great place to start."

Wright didn't respond.

"I'm making my rounds today, introducing myself to those who I'll be working with. I'll see you again soon. It was nice to visit with you today." Dr. Turner stood.

Wright gave a nod and watched as Dr. Turner buzzed out.

PRESENT DAY: Detectives Jewels and Joe

Joe felt tired after watching Jewels all day, a bit like watching a squirrel dashing between stashes of nuts. He got her attention by jangling keys.

"Come on, Jewels. Let's go for a drive," he said.

"Where?"

"You need some time to unwind. To get away from all that." He pointed at her stashes of paperwork on the desk.

"I need to find answers," she said with a sigh.

"And we will," Joe said. "But you also need to relax in order to look at it with fresh eyes."

"Joe." She touched his arm lightly. "You know I can't relax with this monster in our town. He's going to strike again. He's just messing with us for now. I take that as a challenge."

"Yes, of course," Joe said. "But that's part of his plan, Jewels. He's banking on us wearing ourselves out so that we can't see the obvious. Look, I'm not saying stop. I'm saying take a small break, okay?"

"Yeah, fine." Her voice was resigned. "Let me grab my purse."

Joe sat behind his assigned vehicle and waited for Jewels to settle in. They buckled up and pulled out of the station. He headed east.

"Are we going anywhere in particular?" Jewels asked.

"No. We're just unwinding. We can go grab a drink. Maybe a bite? I don't think you've stopped to do either since you got here. You just need to get away from it just for a bit."

"If we grab something to eat, then can we go back?"

"Yes, as long as it's not McDonald's."

Her shoulders slumped, and he could not suppress a smile.

"Let's go to The Buzz Cafe. They're known for good home-cooking."

"Well, it's getting late. What about Kaylee?"

Joe shrugged. "She'll be home a bit late. She's going to eat with some friends. She's a big girl now. Besides, I texted her to tell her I'd be out, too; that we're working hard on a case."

Jewels nodded. "Sure, then. I just don't want to take you away from your family more than I already do."

"Jewels. I do what I do because I choose to. My wife and daughter understand and support me. It's because of us they sleep better at night."

"I guess." She looked out her window.

"Stop feeling guilty. You're the one I'm worried about."

"Because I don't have a family?"

"In a way, yes. You push yourself and push yourself. Being passionate is one thing, but going without

44

sense is another. You've got to take care of yourself, Jewels. This isn't the first time I've told you that."

Her eyes slid over to him. "I *am*."

"Oh, really? How many hours did you sleep last night?"

Jewels shrugged. "I don't know."

"Um, hum. Did you go to bed at all?"

"Yes."

"Pretty evasive responses. How much sleep did you get?"

Jewels got out of the car, and Joe followed her into the diner. They were seated at a table with cushioned black chairs. Joe's hazel eyes were studying Jewels when she looked up.

"Well?" he asked.

"Look, Joe, I just can't sleep. I feel like I need to be doing something to crack this case. How can I sleep with that on my head?"

"Perspective, my dear. You can't give your full focus to something when you're not one hundred percent. If you don't take care of you, then you can't take care of anything else."

The server appeared and took their orders.

"Just give me the turkey club, please, and maybe an order of fries," Jewels said. "Oh, and coffee."

Joe's brows raised.

"And a water with lemon," she added.

"I'll take the Black and Blue Burger, cooked medium, with fries," Joe said. "And a Diet Coke."

"I'll be back with your drinks," the server said.

Jewels fiddled with the saltshaker. "How do you do it, Joe?"

"Do what?"

"Hold it together. I know you're just as passionate about cases as I am, but you've got a wife and a kid. How do you do it?" She finally put the shaker down and looked up at him.

"One step at a time," Joe said. "I have to put things in perspective. That's what you've got to learn, too, or this job will eat you alive. Some things you can't leave at work. It just follows you home, but you can't live and breathe it, Jewels. You can at work, but you've got to try to leave work at work."

"I don't know how."

"I know. Some of that is what makes you so good, but for your own sake, you're going to have to learn a bit more balance."

"But *how*?" Her eyes pleaded more than he thought possible.

"I have some ideas, but you won't like them."

Her lips curved up as she guessed his answer. "Okay, besides getting a boyfriend."

Joe laughed. "It would definitely help to draw your attention more to fun and relaxation rather than living and breathing cases all the time."

"I may need some distraction, but not that much," she said and laughed.

Joe chuckled. "See, now I like the sound of your laugh. I don't hear it often enough. Just talking about a boyfriend already made you lighten up."

"You're impossible. Okay, besides a love interest, how do I achieve this elusive balance you're speaking of?"

"You've got to get interests besides cases, Jewels. Get a dog or cat. Go to the gym. Read a book that isn't about murder or procedures. I don't know." Joe pulled at his ear. "Paint. Get an adult coloring book. Hell, do *something* to take you mentally away for a bit of time."

"Oh, I guess that might work," she said dubiously. "Geez. I don't even know what I'm interested in." She bent forward and ran her fingers into her hair on both sides of her head. She pressed into them as she stared at the table.

"Look, maybe Cara and I can help you. You may not like what we do, but then again, you might. How about we take you to a movie? I've also been meaning to plan a bowling night for the department. Let's say you give those things a try."

Jewels nodded. "Sure. I'll give it a go."

A short while later, their orders arrived.

"Joe, I don't even have any friends outside of you and Cara. I mean, sure, I like everyone at the department, but you couldn't call us... friends, could you?"

"It depends. I have people I consider friends that we don't really connect with all that often, but the important thing is that you *do* connect. It takes an effort on both ends. I think you'll find you do have friends, but you just need to ask them to join you on some fun activities."

"Okay."

"Outside of the precinct, Jewels."

"Gotcha. Let's start all this with a movie and bowling. But can we... start after this case?"

Joe just shook his head.

PRESENT DAY: Wylie

One of the new missions Wylie had assigned himself without realizing it was Detective Polten. He found himself in her shadows more and more. He watched as the two detectives on his case worked together at the police station, visited scenes and places together, and ate together. For some reason, it bothered him.

Just who was this man to Detective Polten? Yes, Joe was her partner, but he was something more. They certainly weren't lovers. Wylie would know if they were. Was it merely a friendship? The clone shook his head. *What was it then?* A strange feeling welled up.

Wylie stood directly behind Joe in the diner. Part of him wanted to kill the man. It would remove Joe from the detective's life, but then he wondered how deeply it would affect her. Part of his fascination with the attractive brunette was how deeply she cared. It

48

motivated and drove her to find answers. Wylie felt like it drew them closer together.

The invisible soldier grinned when he imagined the two of them closer still. He took a few steps. At this point, he was standing directly behind Detective Polten as she finished her meal with Joe. In fact, he reached out a hand and touched a strand of her hair as she lifted her glass of lemon water to drink.

Suddenly, the cloned man realized how he'd made a first. *Was he actually considering how his actions would affect another?* He drew in a breath and staggered a step with the realization. To his surprise, he accidentally kicked a chair.

PRESENT DAY: Detectives Jewels and Joe

"Did you hurt your toe, Joe?" Jewels asked with a grin. She was amused at the force from which the chair had flown to the side. It had moved several feet. "Is Restless Leg kicking in?"

"No, it wasn't me. Did you hurt yourself?" He smiled back. "To make the chair fly that far out, that had to sting just a little bit."

"I didn't do that," she snickered. "Don't try blaming me."

Joe's smile faded. "Jewels. I seriously didn't do that."

"Well, who did it then? If it wasn't you, and it wasn't me? Chairs don't just move like that on their own."

They stared at each other a moment before rising. As the partners were walking out, Jewels paused to look back at the table. Her face wore a measured look.

PRESENT DAY: Wylie

Wylie knew the detective's expression well enough to understand that she was still calculating what the cause of the chair movement could have been. He shrugged to himself and waited a few minutes before exiting the building.

TWO YEARS SIX MONTHS AGO: Army Lab

Dr. Turner watched several lab technicians closely as they stared at monitors doing data analysis. Mathew brought in a few promising candidates, for he wished to recruit one or two to help him on a more... personal study.

Denten Smith caught his interest. The kid reminded him more and more of his daughter who refused to even consider working with him. Not only were they in the same age bracket, but both possessed an innocent enthusiasm about discovery that was intriguing. Gritting his teeth, he purposely walked toward the young man.

"Denten."

The young man with sandy-colored hair looked at his supervisor. "Yes, sir?"

"How would you like to work with me as my personal technician? You have a lot of what I'm looking for in an assistant."

"Sir!" His brown eyes lit with excitement.

"If you're interested, come with me."

Denten followed the older man from the lab. The other technicians glanced up before resuming their tasks. Mathew led the young man into an office.

"Have a seat."

Denten sat, as did the doctor.

"How good are you at... keeping secrets?"

"Sir?"

"This work ... is very... secretive. I'm talking top military clearance."

"Oh, sir, I can definitely keep my mouth shut."

"You'd have to sign your life away to guarantee this. You up for it?"

"May I ask what all this involves?"

"Your job, at this point, is simply to study brain waves of death row inmates. Look for patterns that seem... odd or abnormal. I can't say more until you agree to work with me."

Denten stood with his eyes wide. "Sir, I jump at the opportunity. Please, consider me your man."

"Let me get those non-disclosure agreement forms. If, at any point, you do not want to proceed, you cannot speak of this work to anyone. Not family, not friends. No one, young man. You don't want the Army looking for you."

Denten's skin paled, but his bright eyes remained avidly focused. He shifted in his seat and grabbed the edges of the chair as if to hold himself down. With effort, he swallowed.

"Understood sir. I'll sign those forms as soon as you get them to me."

Dr. Turner stood, grabbed the documents, and placed the papers in front of his new assistant. Denten's face split into a wide grin.

TWO YEARS FIVE MONTHS AGO: Army Interview Office

Denten stood outside the Army office and breathed in and out slowly. His heart was racing. He wondered what kind of training he was in for.

The portal suddenly swung open. A tall man with nearly black hair was standing before him in a dress uniform. He had startlingly blue eyes.

"Denten Smith?"

"Uh, yes, sir."

"Come in."

Denten walked into the office. At first glance, the office and furniture were a harsh contrast to what he was used to. Although modern, the chairs were thin and hard.

The colonel walked to a table and gestured toward a chair. "Sit."

Denten sank slowly onto the cold fabric while the officer settled on the opposite side.

"You want to work with Dr. Turner."

"Yes, sir." Denten swallowed.

"There's a process to that. I'm Colonel Landers, and I'll be heading up your... assessments for the next few days."

Denten nodded before he could choke out another, "Yes, sir."

"Normally, a person of lower rank would be... handling this process, but the general has personally asked me to head this up. You've passed your background check and completed your Standard Form 86. The next step is an interview. I'll be asking you quite a few questions. Then we'll do a few personality tests and scenario questions. From there, the general will decide whether you graduate. Dr. Turner says you've already signed the non-disclosure agreements."

"Yes, sir."

"Do you require anything before we begin?"

"No, sir."

"Okay. Tell me about your hat."

"Excuse me, sir? You want to know about my ball cap?"

"Yes." Hard blue eyes tightened minutely.

Denten licked his lips under the unnerving stare. "It was a gift from my father, sir. He was a pilot, you see. He took me to a Baltimore Orioles game just before he was killed in an accident."

"That's why you wear it all the time."

"Yes, sir."

"Tell me about your father."

"Is... this part of the interview... sir?" Denten asked.

"You could say that."

"Well, he really didn't discuss his job with me in detail because... I suppose, because I was a kid."

"A kid in med school."

"Yes. But, I prefer the technical end. Uh, how did you know?"

"Go on."

"Well, he was a pilot. Not for commercial planes, but I think he ran medications all over the United States. Sometimes, he flew into other countries to pick up orders. He was a good man who cared about people. That's basically all I know, sir."

The general nodded. "Did you ever go with him?"

"On occasion. Just to keep him company."

"What countries did your father typically visit?"

"Um, Canada, France, Germany. I'm not sure of everywhere he went, sir."

"Do you or any in your family believe in Communism?"

Denten's eyes widened. "No, sir."

"Have you ever in the past or present done illegal drugs?"

"I, uh, was caught smoking a joint in the parking lot of a bar a few years ago. But..." Denten rushed to push out the words, "nothing since then, I swear."

"Have you ever been arrested?"

"No, sir."

The Colonel scribbled something on his pad.

"Your neighbors say you're a quiet man. Mind your own business."

Denten inhaled. "You've... talked to my neighbors?"

"Why wouldn't we?" the colonel asked. "You're applying to work with top secret military data with SCI clearance. Surely you knew we'd thoroughly check you out."

"Oh, yes, sir. I figured that, but I'm not asking to be a bodyguard for the president. I'm just a little surprised is all."

"Young man. The Army has a mighty sword to carry. We protect and serve the people of the United States of America. Whether that's in a laboratory or in a war zone, we take top security information *very* seriously. When you sign up, you could be saving a life at the sacrifice of your own. There are many, many secret projects run by our government, and there *are* certain risks involved."

"Yes, sir. I apologize, sir."

The officer gave a curt nod. After another hour of intense questioning, the colonel stood.

"Go stretch your legs and grab a drink. There's a cooler at the end of the hall. I'll meet you back here in fifteen. I'll be giving you the TAPAS, a military personality test, and I'd like to see how you do on the Rorschach Ink Blots."

"Yes, sir."

The door to Colonel Landers office was open when Denten reported the next day. Denten stood at the door uncomfortably, unsure whether he should enter without the command.

"You're prompt. That's what I like to see," said the Army officer, seeming to appear suddenly from within the room. "Come in."

Denten returned to his seat from the day prior.

"Today we'll begin with a few scenarios. Then we'll briefly discuss a summative of your personality tests. After that, you'll meet the big man. He'll have the final say on your hire."

"Yes, sir," Denten said quietly.

"Okay. The first scenario is that you are a doctor, capable of healing. A client comes to you and needs surgery to live, but the chance of surviving the surgery is 15%. What do you do?"

"I'd operate, sir," Denten said with no hesitation.

The colonel scribbled on his pad.

"Your mother is dying without needed medication which she can't afford. You work for a pharmacy. Do you steal the medicine to help her survive?"

"Yes, sir."

The pen scrawled on the page.

"You are a doctor who's discovered a new vaccine. It could save millions of lives but hasn't had the testing background to pass the FDA. In a trial test, it killed 40% but cured 60%. Do you continue to test?"

"Yes, sir."

"Why."

"Because it helps more than it hurts, sir."

Landers wrote more.

"You are ordered to stay put. To stay where you are, and to trust. Then the house catches on fire. Do you stay or go?"

"I am unsure, sir. I feel like in that situation, I wouldn't know what I'd do until that moment."

"I like your honesty," the officer said as he wrote.

"If your supervisor told you to do something questionable in the name of progress, would you?"

"I believe so, sir."

"Good. So I believe I have enough information to go to the general on you. Your personality results basically show the same results as I've determined here today."

"Sir?"

"You are even-tempered and intelligent. You listen to authority and are cooperative. Your self-control is good. You're tolerant and optimistic overall. You're willing to try new things, even questionable things, to help improve our world. These are admirable traits in this line of work."

Denten smiled for the first time. "Thank you, sir."

"Dismissed for today. Show back up tomorrow at 1000 hours."

"Yes, sir."

<><><><><>

General Hawkins sat at his desk. He picked up the phone and punched in a number. "Bring him in."

Denten found himself escorted into an office deep in the heart of the fort. Finally, after what seemed like miles of walking, the colonel pushed him through a heavy portal.

"Sit," said a large man behind the desk. He wore a dress uniform with four stars on both shoulders.

"General Hawkins, this is Denten Smith."

Denten found himself under the scrutiny of the powerful man. Finally, the general said, "Denten, you've passed your drug screening and all other assessments we've asked of you. Before I offer you this position, however, I do have a few more items of discussion."

"Yes, sir."

The general's beady eyes swung to the colonel. "Does he know?"

"Sir, no sir."

"Denten, I think you should be aware that we knew your father."

Denten slowly nodded as he absorbed the information.

"Do you want to know in what capacity?"

"Yes, sir."

The general stood and walked over to a bookshelf. His back was to the young man.

"On occasion, we'd hire your father's services. He'd fly to get us… ingredients for new medications we needed. He also was under oath of no disclosure. Don't take it hard that you didn't know."

The general turned back and leveled a stare. He threw a picture on the table. It was of his father being presented a certification by the general.

"We know all about you and your family, and we feel you'd make a good fit here."

"Th - thank you sir."

"What you're going to see when you, ah, help Dr. Turner are some novel ideas. Some might not agree with what we're trying to do here, but it's for the betterment of society, specifically, our country. Do you think you can handle concepts on the brink of what most value as moral?"

"Yes, sir. I'm most willing to help America advance." Denten adjusted his hat.

"One more thing." Denten received the full weight of the general's stare.

"Yes, sir?"

"Under no circumstances will we tolerate betrayal. Our arms are very long."

Denten swallowed. "Understood."

"Welcome aboard."

TWO YEARS FIVE MONTHS AGO: Secret Army lab

The room was pristine. It held no color or contagions. The patient had receptors glued to his skin, and the beeps of the machines recorded his body's systems. The man's eyes fluttered open, and his pupils adjusted to the harsh lights. When he attempted to move, he found he was handcuffed to his hospital bed.

"How are you feeling, Wright?" asked a man in a white lab coat.

He blinked several times, then asked hoarsely, "Dr. Turner?"

"Yes."

"Wh – where am I? What happened?" Wright asked. His eyes still explored the bland room.

"You're in a facility. A lab deep in the heart of a military base," Dr. Turner replied with a smile.

"But," Wright asked, "Why am I here? Did something happen?" He paused to consider what the doctor said. "Wait... in a lab? Not a hospital?"

"You were not injured if that's what you mean," Dr. Turner consoled. "Look, Wright. Most people don't want to die. I'm trying to learn how to beat death... with your help."

"How can I help?" asked Wright in surprise. "I'm waiting to die."

"That's precisely why I chose you," the doctor said with a little smile.

"You're not making any sense," Wright said, rattling the handcuffs against the bars of the bed.

"I inserted a chip in the base of your skull," the doctor stated with a proud smile. "It'll monitor your body's vibrations during your waking hours and during the different phases of sleep. I believe that this is how we can bring you back to life after your execution."

"Um, Doc, that's a little crazy. Why would they execute me in the first place just to bring me back to life?" Wright asked. "And that's bullshit that you chipped me." Wright's face grew redder as he thought about it. "I didn't even get asked if that was okay. And let me be clear; it's not."

"We really had no choice..." Dr. Turner began.

"You mean I had no choice, right?" Wright growled.

"No," Dr. Turner admitted, "You didn't have a choice. But in the end, it'll save your life."

"Want to bet on that?" said Wright through gritted teeth.

"Look, if I can figure out what I need from you, I can bring you back to life. You'll be reborn into a new body." exclaimed Dr. Turner. His eyes flashed with his passion.

"Who says I want a new body?" Wright asked. His brows formed mad V's as he spoke.

"Well, there's no choice on the matter," Dr. Turner said unsympathetically.

"The damn government thinks this is okay?" asked Wright. "You're saying I have about as much rights as a dog?"

"I don't know why you wouldn't be happy at a second chance," Dr. Turner said, ruffled. "You'd have a blank slate, born back into life as a man without a cage."

"You might want to pick a different guinea pig, Doc. If you don't get this fucking chip out of my neck, you'll be sorry."

"I – uh, I have to wait until you heal before the procedure can be reversed," Dr. Turner said. "The swelling complicates an immediate reversal. It could cause brain damage."

"As soon as it's safe, you get this computer chip outta me, Doc, or you'll pay. You won't want to bring me back from the other side, I can promise you."

TWO YEARS FOUR MONTHS AGO: Secret Army Lab

Denten stood in the doorway of the secret Army lab. It was his first day on the job after his intense questioning by the high-ranking military officials.

His eyes darted around the room, and small beads of sweat lined his upper lip. He felt honored to be chosen for a top-priority clearance study, but he wondered if any part of it would be dangerous.

"There you are," said Dr. Turner. He met him at the door, smiling. He laid a hand on his shoulder and guided him to a desk with rows of monitors. Each screen was divided into quarters; each section featuring an inmate.

"Have a seat."

"What do you -"

"Give me a minute, and I'll explain," Dr. Turner said with a chuckle.

Denten settled into the comfortable chair. He looked at the men on the screens. "These must be the inmates you mentioned."

"Yes. I'm very interested in what happens inside their brains as they sleep. That's what you'll be monitoring."

Denten looked up in surprise. "Is that it, sir?"

Mathew said, "Oh, there's a lot more to it, but this is where you'll begin. I want you to study their sleep patterns. Look for anything that falls away from what you'd expect to see. Watch for spikes or dips in body temperature, readings, or anything surrounding REM and non-REM sleep. If you find *anything*, anything at all, document your observations and alert me."

"So, I'll just be sitting here reading monitors or printouts of their brainwaves, then?"

Again, Dr. Turner patted him on the shoulder. "Son, this is a very *very* important turning point in my life's research. This is ground-breaking stuff... You seem a little tense."

Denten cleared his throat and tried to form a smile. "I - I didn't know what to expect, sir. If this would be dangerous... or anything."

"No, it shouldn't be dangerous, but what I'll eventually expose you to is unbelievable. When I divulge the basis of our purpose here, you'll feel like you're living in a science fiction novel. If we can find what I know is here, we'll be rich and infamous."

"Okay." Denten said with bright eyes. "I'll do my best to find what you're looking for, sir. When do I start?"

Dr. Turner looked at him with his brows raised. "Be my guest." Mathew bowed very slightly and held his hand out to the monitors.

"Sir? I won't be able to read anything until they get their electrodes."

Mathew laughed. "There aren't any."

"What? How will I read the brainwaves then?"

"At night, when these guys sleep," Dr. Turner waved a hand absently at the monitors, "I can measure their body frequency through these devices." He picked up a tiny microchip from a full container.

Denten took the chip from the doctor and turned it over in his hand. His eyes widened suddenly. "A microchip?"

Grinning, Dr. Turner nodded.

"They, ah, didn't mind?" asked Denten. His brows raised as he looked at the doctor.

Dr. Turner laughed. "They're the scourge of society. They don't have the right to decide if I experiment on them or not," he said. "What I'm doing doesn't interfere with their quality of life."

Denten shrugged and nodded once. "You may be crazy, but I guess you're the boss."

The doctor's laugh echoed around the nearly empty room. It was a little louder and longer than before.

ONE YEAR AGO: Secret Army Lab

Denten stooped over the screen. He sat up straight and leaned in for a better view.

"Doctor Turner!" he said, waving emphatically.

Dr. Turner rapidly approached. His eyes squinted slightly and didn't waver during his approach.

"Yes, Denten? Did you find something?"

"Yes, sir. Finally. You asked me to let you know if I found anything... different."

"Right. With the REM and non-REM sleep patterns, I assume? What did you find?"

Denten nodded.

"What did you find?"

"Well, sir, if you look at this data, you'll see before REM sleep, the body's temperature frequency comes down, just a tiny dip, and right at the end of REM sleep, it takes a short hiccup back up. It seems to be consistent across all subjects *All* the inmates, sir."

"By God, Denten! This is exactly what I was hoping to find." Dr. Turner clapped. "It's genius, my boy!"

"What does it mean, Doctor?" Denten asked.

"It means you're going to have all the women you've ever wanted, son. Because you're working with me, you get to ride my coattails to fame and fortune."

Denten watched as Dr. Turner did a happy dance around the monitors and adjusted his ball cap.

TEN MONTHS AGO: Secret Army Lab

When Denten walked into the lab, he noticed a new machine. It was the size of a laptop but a bit bulkier. It was black with a large red button in the middle. Dr. Turner sat in front of it and two larger monitors.

"We've got it," said Dr. Turner. He acknowledges his assistant with a slight nod, but his eyes never left the devices. "Come see."

Denten drew closer. One screen showed an inmate sleeping in solitary confinement, and the other displayed a strange green and yellow iridescent splash of energy. As it shifted, hints of rainbow hues shimmered before melting back into green and yellow.

Denten leaned closer, staring intently at the monitor with the green and yellow shimmers. A minuscule shiny silver string stretched across both monitors from the energy to the man's head.

Dr. Turner's face glistened, and his body was tense. He pointed to the sensor tracking the green and yellow colors. "This is soul energy you're seeing."

"Wow. That's soul energy?" Denten leaned in even more. "How are you able to track that, sir? I mean, life energy isn't physical."

"This is partly your discovery, Denten. I assigned the research, but this is what you found." Dr. Turner smiled.

Denten adjusted his hat and beamed at his supervisor. "Those hiccups before and after REM sleep."

"Yes, son. This device is incredibly special." Mathew patted the black machine. "Those hiccups surrounding REM sleep gave me the idea for this finishing touch. I was able to design a program that can mark the soul's resonation with a magnetic number. I just didn't know how to achieve this until your discovery."

"This is what's going to make us rich, sir?"

Mathew laughed. "Oh, so very. More than your wildest dreams. Okay, so with the first hiccup, the soul leaves the body. That's when I stamp it with the magnetic marker. Now, I have that man's soul frequency, so I, uh, can track it."

The two men watched the energy for a bit. Mathew noted the younger man's fascination as he absorbed every change on the monitors.

"Denten. There's a lot more you should know. My daughter didn't appreciate my genius, but I can tell you do." The doctor paced. "No one else has done what I have."

"I'm ready to know more, sir. You can tell me everything."

"I'm sure you've read the theories about astral travel, right?"

"Yes, I know about that, sir."

"I'll start off by saying it's true. Souls rejuvenate during this time. The soul has a natural marker. I believe it makes the body vibrate with a one-of-a-kind sound. This song, if you will, provides the soul with guidance back to the body before waking."

"So, you're saying... the vibrational frequency is a magnet to bring the soul back home?"

Dr. Turner nodded. "Correct. It's each person's signature."

Dr. Turner touched the silver thread on the screen from one monitor and traced it to the other.

"Do you see this?" he asked.

"Now I do," Denten said, squinting at the monitor.

"That's what the frequency looks like; a projection we can see. This man is sleeping, so his soul is rejuvenating during REM sleep. When he wakes, everything on this monitor will disappear."

"Are you going to sell this information, sir? Is that how we'll get rich?"

Mathew laughed again. "Such enthusiasm for wealth. Not quite. Remember how I told you the Army was involved?"

"Yes."

"Well, I was hired based on my past work and published studies. You've met General Hawkins. He provided me with money, a lab, and subjects for the next step... for what we've done here. But it's only half of the equation. When this man is executed?" Mathew tapped the screen of the sleeping man.

"Yes?" Denten said breathlessly.

"There is a collection of men waiting for souls."

"What?" Denten asked as he straightened. He also paced, repeatedly putting his hat on and taking it off. "Sir, how can that be?"

"The Army has clones, but they are just the shells, not really alive ... yet. General Hawkins hired me to find life forces for them. We have bodies without souls, so why not use souls that no longer have bodies?"

Denten's mind was whirling. "The death row inmates. Brilliant! So... Clones? Like, for war? Super soldiers?"

Mathew nodded with a huge smile. "We just discovered how, son. And eventually, that is how the money will roll in."

Finally, Denten turned to the monitor depicting the greens and yellows of the inmate's soul and said, "Wow.

You're right about it feeling like… fiction. We'll get to see this happen since this is our work, right? I mean, when that man is executed, we'll be able to watch his soul transfer to a clone?"

"You bet! When I push this button," Dr. Turner said, indicating a red control, "it replicates the soul's frequency. If pushed while that man was alive, his soul wouldn't know which place to go."

Denten's mouth dropped, and he drew in an excited breath. "Couldn't that kill him, sir? But that means we wouldn't have to wait until his execution to use his soul, then."

"I suppose that's true," Dr. Turner said, chuckling. He patted Denten's back. "But we don't want to be infamous for murder, now, do we? We'll just wait until his time is up to transfer his energy."

"Yes, sir." His shoulders slumped just enough for the doctor to notice. "Sir, I have another question."

"Go on."

"Do you really want to reincarnate death row inmates?"

"Why not?" Doctor Turner asked. "They love killing." He shrugged.

"True, but murderers aren't known for conformity. They… wouldn't go on killing… like kill civilians, would they?"

"The cloned bodies have the capacity to use a soldier's mind," Dr. Turner said, "Their natural love of discipline should override the soul's desire for chaos."

"I hope you're right, sir."

"Well, it *is* an experiment, so there'll be trial and error. If it helps, reincarnates have no memory of prior lives."

"How do you know?"

Dr. Turner said simply, "Do you remember your past life?"

"So, you believe their souls are corrupt. You're saying that although they won't remember their past life, their soul will continue the desire to kill, making them perfect for assassins."

Mathew chuckled. "Preachers may not agree with me, but yes. I believe souls retain their basic level of development from one life to the next. These men," he waved to the scores of inmates on the monitors, "have not finished their life's purpose. Basically, in their next life, they will pick up where they left off... without the memories. See this man sleeping?" Dr. Turner tapped on the image of the inmate and looked at his technician.

"Yes. That's Wright Miller. He's the first of our subjects scheduled for execution."

"Right. It could be next week, or it could be in six months. But you'll get to see the entire thing."

Denten's eyes regained their shine. He grinned and tossed his hat up high.

EIGHT MONTHS AGO: Private inmate meeting room

Wright was brought into a small square room; brick painted off-white. Plexiglass over the barred windows offered some privacy. It was a place for lawyers to meet with their clients.

The officers sat Wright in a metal chair. His shackles were attached to anchors in the room, and his wrists to the chair. A rectangular table was between him and another chair. All furniture items were secured.

The door buzzed and Dr. Turner entered. "Thank you, officers. I'll take it from here."

The men nodded and said, "Just buzz us when you're finished, Doc."

The door closed and the magnetic lock clicked.

"Hello, Wright," the doctor said with a smile. He sat opposite the
man.

Wright sat gloomily. His narrowed gaze settled on the figure in the white lab coat. His brows were knitted, and his face a stormy hue.

"Now, don't be like that," Dr. Turner said. "I'm here to help."

"Fuck you." Wright hissed through his pressed lips.

"Come now," the doc tried to soothe. "Your time here on Earth is nearly up, but that's only for this body."

"Doc, I've given you many opportunities to stop what you're doing to me. You've ignored my demands to have this fucking chip removed. If you continue with your experiment on me, you won't like the results."

"What could it hurt, my boy?" asked Dr. Turner. "You're facing death, but you can open your eyes in a young, strong body."

"I'm facing death no matter what," Wright said. "Doc, you already know you can't fix me. I like to kill."

"Your murders have been for revenge," the psychologist replied. "You just need an outlet. You can be an assassin for the military in your new life. Think of it, paid to kill people."

Wright slammed his fists on the arms of the chair. It echoed through the little room.

"Get it through your fucking head, doc. I won't be controlled. I won't be manipulated. I kill because I *want* to kill, and I hold grudges. If you value your life... or your daughter's, you'll reconsider. I don't think either of you want to end up on my dinner plate. I will not be an employee for the people who took away my free choice."

Dr. Turner said, "Wright, you probably won't remember who you were in this life anyway, so I really don't care what you think you want or don't want. You pissed away your choices when you decided to gut people you hated and got locked up."

Wright tried to leap to his feet and was frustrated by the chain. His veins were outlined in his neck and his eyes bulged with anger. The noise of the chains scattered the quiet. Dr. Turner moved back slightly, trusting the chains.

"Your execution date is in one week," Dr. Turner said, standing. "I'll see you, or should I say, Wylie, on the other side... of the prison that is." He smiled and then hit the buzzer.

PRESENT DAY: Detectives Jewels and Joe

Something awoke Jewels from a deep sleep. She couldn't put her finger on it, she felt as though she was being watched.

A visual sweep of the room reassured her for now. No threats at the moment. The alarm on her phone would go off in about an hour. Jewels threw back the covers and slipped on house shoes. In the kitchen, she started a cup of coffee. While waiting on the brew, she leaned on the counter and absently ran her fingers through her hair.

Soon, her body reactions slowed, and an air of calm returned. Jewels sat at the table and sipped her coffee while she considered becoming less... full-time detective. *What can I do to make more of a personal connection with people?*

As Jewels pulled open the front door, a bright yellow bag of lemons resting against the portal spilled into the entrance way, nearly tripping her.

"What the?" she muttered. "Oh, that Joe. He's being funny and telling me I order too many lemons for my water." She chuckled. The detective picked up the bag and put it in the bottom drawer of her refrigerator. Then she locked the front door and slipped into her car.

On the way to work, Jewels pulled into the donut shop, parked, and walked in.

"Four dozen, please," she said to the clerk.

The young man smiled broadly.

I know what you're thinking, she thought and smiled back, *and you're not that far off.*

The clerk handed her the boxes packed into two large paper bags. "Here you go, officer."

Jewels didn't bother to correct him about her title and tipped him ten dollars. She smiled as his eyes widened.

"Hey, thanks!"

"You bet. Have a good day," she said as she headed out the door.

Eight minutes later, Jewels hauled the goodies in the precinct and set them out on a long table. Satisfied they were sufficiently spread for optimum availability, she cupped her hands to her mouth to make the announcement.

"Donuts, everyone."

"Great. Thanks, detective," called several officers who rushed to gather around the boxes. A few men smiled and nodded appreciation with cheeks full of the pastries.

"You're welcome."

Joe waited for the table congestion to fade away before he grabbed a freshly made glazed donut. "Aren't you going to eat one, Jewels?"

"Nah. I just wanted to be nice. I'll probably grab a cup of bad coffee over there, though," she said and walked toward the pots of black brew. Joe walked with her.

"It's pretty strong," he stated.

Jewels smiled. "Yes. It'll put hair on your chest."

"What about your head?" he asked. He ran a hand over his crown. She laughed as he'd intended.

They both poured cups of coffee.

"So, uh, thanks for the lemons," Jewels said. "It made my morning. I'll try not to order so many for my water next time." She gave a slight chuckle.

"Lemons? You're thanking me for lemons?" Joe looked down at her and grinned.

"Didn't you leave me a bag outside my front door recently?" she asked.

"Not that I recall. Maybe you have a secret admirer."

"Hum." Jewels fell silent. They sipped on their coffees and began to walk toward their desks.

"When do you want to head over to The Disease Center?" Joe asked.

"Let me go through my notes and check my calls. In about an hour?"

Joe nodded.

Both returned to their desks. Jewels pulled out a protein bar and nibbled on it with the strong drink. She compiled a succinct list in her phone of questions she wanted to be sure to ask. Then she began listening to her saved phone messages.

SEVEN MONTHS AGO: Death Row Inmate Cell

A man in a dark suit stood in the corridor. A frayed bible was tucked under his arm. He peered into the cell.

An inmate sat on his thin, hard prison bed. He was leaning over, elbows propped on his knees with his hands clasped in front. For long moments, the man merely looked down without really seeing.

"Hello, Wright. Nice to see you again. Care to chat?"

The man looked up. A sad smile formed on his lips. "Why not? It's not like I have something better to do, Reverend John."

Wright stood. He stretched before walking toward the bars confining him. The preacher pulled up a chair on the outside. He sat where Wright could see him, but he was not within reach. Guards were patrolling and stationed in a few places where they could be seen.

"How are you doing, Wright?" asked Reverend John.

"Well, I could be better." He laughed dryly.

"Yeah, I suppose so. Are you scared?" John asked.

"I don't know. I think I feel more anger than anything."

"Well, anger is based in fear. It's normal to be fearful two days before."

"I know." Wright said. "But it doesn't feel like fear."

"Why do you say you're angry?" The reverend's rich brown eyes looked at him in sincerity.

"Hell… Lots of reasons, Rev. Because I'm here, because I'm going to die in two days, because I can't control myself… which got me here." He paused for a long time. Reverend John let him gather his thoughts. "What in the hell is wrong with me?" Wright sat and raked both hands through his hair. "Oh, and I'm mad at all these fucking doctors."

"They just want to help, Wright. Just in case you get a stay. It's their job."

"Let me ask you something, Rev." The inmate looked up suddenly, blue eyes focused intently on John's hazels.

"Yes?"

"Do you believe in reincarnation?"

Wright continued to stare at the preacher as he awaited a response.

John was silent for a few moments. He gazed upwards as he contemplated his words.

"Christians typically don't believe in reincarnation," he said, "but there is an interesting passage in the Bible. John the Baptist was said to once reside in Elijah. People argue about the meaning of the passage, so take it as you will."

"But do *you* believe in reincarnation?" Wright continued to study the reverend.

"I'm a man of God," he replied. "It's some of the New Agers who believe that."

"Right, so you don't."

"Do *you* believe in reincarnation, Wright? Is that what you're worried about?" The preacher met Wright's light blue eyes.

"I worry about it, yes. And about Karma, you know? Is that real?" he asked.

The preacher thought for a moment. "Again, these concepts can be argued, but as far as Christians are concerned, not really. It's more of an Eastern philosophy."

"Eastern?"

"Yeah, Buddhism, Hinduism, some others."

"Right."

Wright was quiet again. His vision finally shifted away from the preacher.

"I wish I could speak to someone who believes it," Wright said.

"We can talk. Just because I don't believe it doesn't mean I don't know about it."

"Okay... um, thanks."

"You know, I lead a Twelve Step program here. Not all the guys believe in God, but they do believe in their own version of a higher power. A God of their own understanding, we say. God is like that. He comes to each of us in his own way."

Wright nodded. "Okay, so Karma, does it accumulate from life to life? Or is a person born with a blank slate?"

"Well, that depends on which believer you talk to. Buddhists think it accumulates, and we should do good in this life to have a better life next time. Hindus say that Karma is what we do in this life. And if we are good then we come back in a higher life form. If we are not, then we come back in a lower life form. Personally, I don't think Karma would be punishment, per se. I think it's lessons we come here to learn. That's more the Christian view. And if we don't learn from our actions, God gives us the same lessons over and over, giving us the opportunity to change and grow."

"That makes sense, I suppose."

"God says you reap what you sow."

"But don't Christians believe in an Eye for an Eye?"

"Not anymore. That's why Christ came. But, yes. An eye for an eye is a bit like karma."

"So does the terminology matter? If it's the same concept with different religions?" Wright didn't expect an answer and continued. "Anyway, do you believe that souls can be corrupt? What if one can't change no matter how many opportunities are presented?"

"Son, through God, all things are possible. He can move mountains."

"See, I disagree. I've tried to want to change, Rev. I've tried and tried. Maybe the devil is real. I can't get the demon out of me that wants to kill those who've hurt me."

"No one is corrupt who wants to change," the preacher said. "Even the first small step of saying you want it but are unable is progress."

"Well, it's too late for me now. So, you believe I'm going to Hell." Wright cocked a brow.

"But you can repent and accept Christ as your savior. That's why I'm here." The man of God nodded, and the light caught the silver traces in his fine brown hair.

"No thanks, Rev. I don't think it would work if I don't believe in it."

"No, I don't think so either. Maybe we can pray for God to help you believe?"

Wright just laughed. "Okay, let me ask one more question. It's kind of a weird one. Do you think a scientist could create a body, right? And then attract a soul to that body? Like, when a guy dies?"

The preacher smiled. "Clever idea. But, no. I don't think it's possible."

The next evening, a guard brought Wright his last meal.

"This is really gross, man," the guard said. "You wanted this for your last meal? Disgusting."

The guard slid the tray in the slot for that purpose and stood back.

Wright took the tray and put it on the small table. He sat before the covered dish and lifted the lid. He smiled and bent his head over the food and sniffed.

"That is barely cooked," the guard continued.

Wright took his fork and managed to get a piece of the protein on the utensil. Drips of crimson fell onto the plate.

"Rare heart. Just like I like it," Wright said. He smiled when the guard turned away in revulsion.

SEVEN MONTHS AGO: Secret Army lab — Inmate Reincarnation

Denten arrived at a flurry of activity. Dr. Turner had the machinery up and running. One monitor was blank, but the other showed a man being prepared for lethal injection at the prison. Dr. Turner was seated in front of the monitor focused on the inmate.

At first, Denten could see little else. He made a beeline for his supervisor. Dr. Turner briefly acknowledged his arrival with a tiny nod.

Two men in white lab coats escorted a man in fatigues into a chamber. Denten stared. There was something odd about the way the soldier moved. It was very... mechanical.

Turning back to the screen, Denten said, "That's Wright."

"Yes, sir," Dr. Turner answered.

"And that guy must be the clone," Denten made a small motion toward the soldier with the odd gait.

Mathew nodded.

"This is going to be so cool. Watching the very first soul transfer in history."

The doctor laughed good-naturedly.

"Agreed. We'll see the clone, man-made, who can breathe and has autonomic responses, but all somatic responses are controlled by a computer wired directly to his peripheral nervous system, become *alive* once he receives the soul. Then the computer will become unnecessary."

Denten avidly watched as a third doctor brought in a small box and opened it. He stood in front of the clone and took something small and yellow out of the container.

Dr. Turner spoke into a microphone.

"On my mark," he said.

The executioner held up the syringe and tapped it. Dr. Turner said, "Administer Yellow Charge to the clone... Now."

The doctor inserted the capsule into the clone's mouth.

Denten could not stop himself from watching as the lethal injection was administered.

As the poison was dispensed, Dr. Turner hit the red button. The clone's body went rigid then fell to the floor. The soldier had a mild seizure. The two doctors checked his vitals. They spoke to the clone in low tones.

Within minutes, the man moved his hand of his own volition.

Dr. Turner and Denten joined the gathering around the prone man. The soldier blinked in the light and struggled to sit up as he oriented himself.

"Wh – where am I?" he rasped.

"Welcome, Wylie," Dr. Turner said. "Let's help him."

The two men in white lab coats assisted Wylie to his feet.

"You are part of a Defense Department funded program." Dr. Turner explained to the man in fatigues. "You're now a part of a black ops secret missions, soldier. General Hawkins or I will be giving your orders."

"Yes, sir," Wylie said.

Dr. Turner caught Dr. James's attention: huge smiles plastered both of their faces.

Dr. Turner turned and faced him. He said, "We did it, Bellamy."

"Yes. Congratulations to us. Our research will go down in history."

"That and the Yellow Charge formula will make everyone here very rich," Dr. Turner added. He made eye contact with Denten and winked.

Both men laughed, clasped hands, and slapped each other's backs.

"I couldn't be more pleased with the results of this experiment," Mathew said.

"Agreed. Now, all we have left to do is to celebrate!"

The soldier cleared his throat, drawing their attention back to him.

Dr. Turner smiled again and put a hand on Wylie's shoulder. "If you will, Bellamy, take Wylie and help acclimate him."

"Of course," he said. "It's my honor. I'll monitor as he makes the transition and document my findings."

"Thank you. When he's ready, I'd like to prepare Wylie for a mission."

"It won't take long," his close friend said, "We just need to run some tests before we set him free."

Dr. Turner nodded.

They took the newly awakened soldier into another section of the lab.

Mathew turned to his assistant. "Come on, my boy. Let's go. We've got a lot to discuss."

Denten nodded, his face alive with enthusiasm.

PRESENT DAY: Detectives Jewels and Joe

"We'd like to speak to the Chief of Surgery, please," Jewels asked the front desk receptionist at Technology of Tomorrow. She flashed her badge to bypass any run-a-round.

"He is not available," replied the receptionist. She bowed her elaborately braided head and returned to her work.

"Who *is* available we could talk to?" Jewels asked, not bothering to keep the irritation from her voice. She tapped the receiving desk with her short but serviceable nails.

The receptionist gave a perfunctory look and said, "I'll see what I can do." Her dark eyes flashed as she punched numbers into her phone.

Jewels took a seat by her partner and crossed her legs. A short while later, the young woman said, "Dr. Montrose will see you now."

The receptionist stood and led them down a white tiled hallway into a smaller foyer with three doors that led into individual offices.

"If you will sit here, he'll be with you shortly," the young lady said, nodding to the chairs arranged comfortably around the area.

"Thank you," Joe said and sat in a black recliner. A nearby glass coffee table held a scatter of magazines.

After the woman departed, Jewels took in a calming breath and let it out. She'd found the weak smile of the receptionist annoying. She caught a hint of an amused smirk on her partner's face.

Jewels intentionally ignored him and picked up one of the publications about the science of cryogenics. She sat across from Joe on a green leather sofa and flipped through the pages for a few minutes.

"Well, this is interesting," she said.

"What?"

"There's a promotion for a new way to use cryogenics," Jewels said.

"And what's that?" Joe asked.

"Other than freezing sick people for future cures, they're advertising the Fountain of Youth," she replied. She tossed the magazine back on the table.

"How so?"

Jewels said, "If their clients come in weekly for cryogenic treatment, a combination of injections along with a soak in a special formula, it nearly stops the aging process."

"Oh, really?" Joe's interest caught his partner's attention.

Jewels smiled at him and raised her finely arched brows. "Do you want to know as a detective... or as a potential client?"

Joe chose not to answer but leaned forward to peek at the magazine.

Jewels continued, "Yes, and guess who the head scientist on the project was?" She tucked a strand of dark hair behind an ear.

"I'm going to guess Dr. Torrent."

"Bingo." Jewels leaned back in her chair.

One of the wooden portals swung open and a short, slender man stepped forward. He was sharply dressed, about mid-thirties, and his hair was beginning to recede.

"Dr. Montrose?" Joe asked.

"Yes, Mr.?"

"Hi, I'm Detective Combs, and this is my partner, Detective Polten."

The doctor's brows raised and wrinkled his forehead. He cleared his throat and then said, "Nice to meet you. Why don't we talk in my office?"

"Sure."

"Follow me." The doctor turned and walked with stiff indignation back through the door he'd come through.

They stepped through the framed portal into a plush office. Original art pieces by well-known artists hung about the room. A thick, cream imported rug spread comfortably over the deep mahogany floor, and an enormous ornate desk sat by the huge window. With a wave of his hand, the doctor indicated for them to seat themselves in the expensive Italian leather chairs.

"To what do I owe this pleasure?" he asked amiably.

"We're on the 'Eat Your Heart Out Killer' case," Jewels said, laying it out on the table.

"No sweet talk here." the doctor chuckled. "But what does this have to do with me?"

"Maybe nothing." Joe said, "That's what we're here to find out."

"What can you tell us about Dr. Torrent?" Jewels asked.

The doctor's eyes widened slightly, and he slowly took in a deeper breath before expelling it quietly. "I know he was murdered," Dr. Montrose said. "He was also the lead doctor in a study here at Technology of Tomorrow."

"Can you tell us the ins and outs of that study?" Jewels asked.

"I can tell you some... but honestly, I don't know all of it." The doctor said with a sniff.

"Tell us what you do know," Joe encouraged.

"Dr. Torrent was a Cryonicist. I don't know if you're familiar with that terminology, but his main responsibility was to assist terminal patients who request freezing."

"Yes, we have a basic understanding of the term," Joe said. His eyes wandered around the room, searching for any more hints about the man before returning to the medical professional. "Really, the patients are nearly frozen, correct?"

The doctor shifted, and the leather creaked in protest. "Correct. They aren't really frozen, but close enough to count."

"What else?" asked Jewels. She crossed her legs and began to jiggle the top foot.

"Well, Dr. Torrent discovered how to prolong youth, too," Dr. Montrose stated proudly. He smiled and looked at each of the officers.

"Basically, the same process only not as extreme?" asked Jewels.

"There's a bit more to it than that." the doctor said, "but in simple terms, yes."

"Does this, by any chance, help heal the overall health of the client as well?" Jewels pressed.

The doctor's mild surprise indicated she'd guessed correctly. "Why... yes," he said. He began fiddling with a paperweight on his desk.

"So, where do you get the funding for this research?" Joe pressed.

The doctor lowered his head then looked back up. "Look, I'll be taking over now that Dr. Torrent is no longer... able. I haven't read over all his notes yet, but I've seen a good portion. I believe that some of the uses and connections are confidential, but I can say that the military is funding a good portion of the cost."

Joe nodded thoughtfully. Then his eyes met Jewels's.

"Hum. I'd say they're a believer in the healing effects, then," Jewels said.

"I believe they have faith in the program," Dr. Montrose agreed. His eyes darted nervously between the two officers. "That's about all I can tell you on this."

"I understand," Jewels said. She smiled to help put him back at ease.

Joe asked, "Did Dr. Torrent have any clients who weren't satisfied in some way?" He leaned forward.

"I - I'm not sure. I think there might have been a client or two who were disgruntled over the cost of the procedure," Dr. Montrose said, "but I don't think they ever had a treatment, though."

"We're going to need their names," Joe said. He took out his phone and opened a note-taking app.

Jewels noticed the doctor's nervousness. His eyes darted, he continually shifted, and he was starting to sweat.

"So, you think the 'Eat Your Heart Out Killer' may have a connection here?" asked Dr. Montrose with a hard swallow.

"That's confidential," Jewels said with a warm smile. "As soon as we're able, we'll let you know more."

The three stood and shook hands.

"Thank you for your help." Jewels said. She flashed another smile.

"And if you think of anything else, please give us a call," Joe said, offering his card.

"Please, get us those names." Jewels said, "And I know this probably isn't possible, but if there're any military patients that are... questionable in character, their names would also be extremely helpful."

The doctor's eyes darted, and his expression was troubled. "I - I would have to get clearance from the military for that."

"Exactly," Jewels said. "Again, thank you so much for your time."

As soon as they were back in the patrol car Joe said, "What do you want to bet our guy is military?"

"That's precisely what I was thinking," Jewels agreed as she shut the door. "We'll get nowhere with those few clients who didn't have enough money."

"But we still have to check them out." Joe buckled his seat belt and put the car in drive.

"For sure."

PRESENT DAY: Secret Army lab

EPDP, Experimental Product and Development Program, a military program, tied together the cloning lab with The Disease Center and Technology of Tomorrow, all vital contributors to a highly classified formula known as Yellow Charge.

The EPDP was located next to the cloning lab on the base for easy access. Here, Yellow Charge was formulated and produced on a limited basis. The drug was designed to boost the energy, heal systems, and deliver adrenaline-charged strength.

Edwin Wentworth, a thirty-year-old man, was at the height of his career. He was short with dark brown, collar-length hair. His wild eyes flashed behind his glasses. Every movement he made was staccato, like hummingbirds at a feeder.

He was in-charge of the miracle drug after production. Ed did not design Yellow Charge, but he was assigned with dosage and monitoring immediate changes in the subjects. He worked directly under Dr. Bellamy James.

"Did you figure out how many capsules he took?" asked Dr. James, looking up expectantly from his work as the younger man approached.

"An undetermined amount, sir," Ed reported. His lips formed a pinched line.

"I need an estimate." Dr. James met Ed's eyes reproachfully. He flipped through a few pages more on his clipboard.

"Sir, he took approximately eight cases." Ed said quietly.

Bellamy stopped focusing on his papers and looked Ed directly in the eyes. "We need to tighten up security in the EPDP. A lot. Wylie just walked right in and took what he wanted. Do you think you can get a hold of the head of security and find a better place to store this stuff? Just sitting in the locked closet, even with the high level of security in place, isn't good enough for someone with The Chameleon's capabilities."

"Yes, sir. I will get on that right away."

The doctor put the clipboard down on a lab table and focused fully on the technician.

"Do you know what all those pills could do in the hands of Wylie?" he asked calmly. He knew very well that Ed understood. Dr. James hoped to drive the seriousness of the offense home.

Ed said, "Sir. They heal, energize, and give the soldier almost superpowers. The capsules replicate adrenaline qualities and heal all injuries at the same time. Wylie knew what he was doing, sir."

"We have got to track him down." Dr. James demanded. He straightened and looked at Ed again, his face grim.

Ed broke eye-contact to look at the blond man who just walked in. The man walked directly to Ed and said, "It has been confirmed, sir." The two shared a meaningful look. Ed promptly returned his gaze to the doctor and announced, "Sir, his tracker is out."

Dr. James's face darkened explosively. He barked, "Figure out his next target and intercept. Use a dart gun to neutralize. He needs to be back in the lab, pronto."

The man beside Ed said in a small voice, "We're on it, sir." He paused and then blurted, "But, um, sir? The dart won't work if he's on Charge."

Dr. James clenched his fists and studied the ceiling for a moment before replying. Finally, he asked, "Have you checked his last residence?"

The blond nodded, "Yes, sir. He abandoned that location once he removed his tracking device."

"Damn!" He slammed his fist, "If he goes rogue, it endangers our whole project."

"Sir?" Ed began, "Next time, we need to place the chip where he cannot remove it."

"I'm already on it. The next chip will be near the spinal cord, but that doesn't help this time."

Dr. James walked away with long strides.

The blond stepped forward. "Permission to speak, sir."

"Go on." The doctor pivoted dramatically to face the soldier. His lab coat billowed.

"We believe Dr. Teigha may be the next target, sir."

Dr. James's brows shot up. His voice was a little higher than normal when he asked, "The person who designed our chip tracking system? Why do you think so?"

"The subject appears to be targeting people assigned to his project. He's made it clear that he doesn't want another tracker." Then he added, "You could also be on that list, sir."

Dr. James was quiet a moment.

"I want a protection detail. And for Dr. Teigha."

"Yes, sir."

"And call Dr. Montrose. He needs to make an appearance at the EPDP. We need his part to make replacement capsules."

Ed replied quickly, "Yes, sir."

"Do it now."

As Ed turned to leave, the blond man spoke up. "Sir? Before I go, there's something else."

Dr. James took a long breath. "Yes?"

"How long has it been since you've talked with Dr. Turner?" The blond watched the doctor very closely.

Dr. James looked contemplative. "I live and breathe this facility. Dr. Turner and I touch base from time to time, though nothing lately."

"Sir, you should know. Dr. Turner's daughter was a target."

"What?" He blanched.

The man continued, "Sir, we believe Wylie attacked Dr. Turner's daughter."

"That means... oh, God, that means..." The doctor staggered a step.

"Yes. I'm sorry, sir."

Dr. James sat heavily in the nearest chair. He slowly rubbed his brows. The officer took his leave to allow his leader time to mourn for his friend's daughter.

SEVEN MONTHS AGO: First Clandestine Kill Mission

"Soldier?" General Hawkins asked.

The cloned man stood at attention. He responded to commands innately, without military training, his brain replicated from a soldier who followed all orders without question or hesitation.

"Do you feel prepared to begin a mission?" The general stood before the soldier, his stern expression studied the man, looking for any signs of weakness.

"Sir, yes sir," Wylie said.

"And you're aware of all your weaponry and functions we've equipped you with internally?"

"Sir, yes, sir. I've passed all preliminary testing evaluations, sir."

The general nodded. "The doctors and trainer informed me of this, but I wanted to hear it from you. Your name is Wylie, but on a mission, you're to be called 'The Chameleon.' You will use this mode when entering and exiting this facility and while on missions. Do you understand?"

"Sir, yes sir."

"Good. You are to take out this man when he is alone," the General said. He held a picture of a dark-skinned male. "Mohammad Dekheir, recently relocated to the US, is a Sudanese militia leader. His job, while here, is to secure weapons on a large scale from the black market to send back to Janjaweed members. We want him terminated with extreme prejudice."

Wylie took the picture. "Just him, sir? Or his entire entourage?"

"For now, just him. We want it to look natural. I want you to feed him this." The general handed Wylie a small vial of a clear liquid. "It will stop his heart. His death will look like a heart attack."

"Copy that, sir."

"He'll be landing in the Dallas/Fort Worth International Airport in two days. You're to follow him and look for an opportunity. If he stays overnight, you'll go to him in the dark. If no other opportunities arise, follow him into the bathroom."

"Sir, yes sir."

"Word is there's a meeting in Arlington, Texas, near Globe Life Park. Instead of attending the game, they'll meet nearby to discuss weaponry and shipment of purchased items. I don't want there to be any purchased items. If we take out Dekheir, they won't proceed."

"Roger that, Sir."

"Dismissed."

Wylie arrived early. He scoped the airport and possible routes to the stadium. Just as the general said, the party arrived and took a rental Suburban to a hotel near the ballpark.

For hours, Wylie merely watched. No other thoughts but the mission. He was a hawk, and they were prey. He would compile data and use it to strike.

Wylie entered the hotel and then the rooms in stealth mode. They had no deluxe accommodations, likely to avoid drawing attention. The rooms were the farthest from the front desk and secure.

The men didn't do anything alone. There was always a cluster around the target. They spoke Arabic, but Wylie understood the language from a decoder in his brain.

"Who opened the door?" one man asked. He waved emphatically toward the entrance.

"No one is over there," another answered. His eyes narrowed and he drew his weapon.

"Are you telling me it just swung open on its own?"

"Yes. You must not have made sure it was closed."

"It was closed and locked. I did so myself."

The man speaking brushed past Wylie but did not notice the contact. He looked both directions down the hall before closing the door again. This time, he not only locked the door but closed the metal bar.

Dekheir continued as if there were no distractions. "Let us leave at 1:30. This is the time we would depart for a ball game."

"Yes, yes," said one of his men. "The meeting has been arranged."

"Very good."

Wylie silently released the bolt and opened the door a second time.

"What is going on here?" yelled the man who'd locked it.

A handful of men charged into the hall. They ran up and down the corridor. They didn't have weapons drawn, but they were secured under their clothing.

They returned, breathing hard and their eyes wide.

"Did you see anything?" Dekheir asked.

"No. Nothing," said the man.

"Shut it again and stand by it this time," the leader said.

The men talked some more, but Wylie did not find it meaningful. When it was close to time to depart, a few used the restroom. However, the target did not.

When the men left the room, Wylie followed.

The group now spoke English to blend in better.

"You get the car," Dekheir said to the man who stood by the door.

"Of course," he said with a nod.

The rest of the group waited in the commons. There were a few colorful modern couches in the room, but no one sat.

Wylie finally found a tiny window of opportunity when the group left to get in the vehicle. No one was paying attention to any other when they loaded. Dekheir headed to the passenger's front seat.

Wylie stood beside the door as the target opened it. As the man was angling himself to sit, Wylie jerked his head back and poured the vile into his mouth. He clamped his hand over his lips to force him to swallow. Immediately, the man began spasming.

Wylie let him fall to the curb, his knife positioned over Dekheir's chest. The tip of the blade rested against the fabric, but he forced his hand still.

Wylie paused and considered his action.

What just happened? I followed mission orders, and suddenly my knife is at this man's chest? I don't even remember acting until I saw the blade. I was not threatened, so why did I pull the weapon?

Wylie straightened and sheathed the blade.

Whoa, he realized. *I'm thinking - processing my reactions. Before, I merely followed orders with no thought...*

SEVEN MONTHS AGO: Processing the First
Clandestine Mission

"Soldier, I'm not easily impressed. You did an
outstanding job." General Hawkin's face finally broke into
a hint of a smile.

Wylie stood at attention. "Thank you, sir."

"I'll have another mission for you in a week. This one
may be a little more challenging."

"Not a problem, Sir," Wylie said.

"Keep doing what you're doing, and you'll go
far. Dismissed."

PRESENT DAY: Wylie

Wylie's anger rose whenever he thought about the
first days of his reincarnation and how mindless he
was. How dare Dr. Turner think he would not remember...
even as he'd handed the general the reins. He should
have known that as soon as Wylie made his first kill, it'd
crack open the door to his past.

*I terminated with liquid on my first mission, yes, and
not a knife, but knowing I'd ended a man's life was
putting the key in the lock, even if it hadn't yet been
turned. Each mission only turned the key until it flung the
door wide open.*

I suspect the Yellow Charge has something to do with my memory recall, too. It heals everything, even evidently, memory loss from prior lives... at least in my case.

Wylie considered his second mission. *How quickly it had all come pouring back once blood was on my hands.*

SEVEN MONTHS AGO: Second Clandestine Kill Mission

"Soldier." General Hawkins barked.

Wylie snapped to Attention.

"At ease. Are you ready for a new mission?"

"Sir, yes sir." As he stood at Attention again.

"At ease, soldier. We're just going to chat."

Wylie stood at Parade Rest.

General Hawkins continued. "This one's more challenging. You'll be required to use more of your technology."

"Will it be an in-country target, sir?" His heart thumped a little faster with the idea of a kill mission.

"Yes, it is. There is a major drug lord in Chicago causing... trouble. You'll be solo on this."

"Roger that. Is their entire operation to be... shut down, Sir?" Wylie said.

"Yes. We want to test your capabilities."

"Understood, Sir."

"If you fail?" The general paused, "you will return to the lab for... fine tuning, let's say."

Wylie stood quietly with a bit of a smirk. The general handed Wylie a file from his desk. In it, Wylie saw images of a man, presumably the drug-lord holding an M4.

"You're looking at Miguel Salazar. He runs operations in the U.S. for the Sinaloa Cartel. He's your target. Terminate with extreme prejudice."

"Take out his stronghold too, sir?"

The general smiled. "I like your confidence, son. He is the main objective. Take advantage of every target opportunity. I am sure there will be plenty. Whatever we can do to shut down their operation. In addition to huge shipments of cocaine and marijuana they also move weapons and launder their funds internationally. He is wanted around the world. We will get to him first, though. Right? We want to send a message to the cartel and to the world. We have it under control. However, it cannot be connected with the U.S. military."

"Copy that."

"They have military grade weaponry." Hawkins turned to face Wylie. "Their weapons are... state-of-the-art. Technically just possessing them is considered an act of war. That is, we are within our rights to simply eliminate them and enemy combatants. We are especially concerned about the ammo they acquired. They have Electro Rounds."

"Sir?"

"In other words, if you get shot, your body turns to ash, but the surrounding area will not ignite. Of course, with Yellow Charge, you won't be in danger."

"Will the rounds deflect with magnetic force like I can do with normal bullets, sir?"

"We believe so, Soldier, but if you're shot in the back, you'll be dead if you don't take Yellow Charge."

"Copy that. How often do I need to take the formula?" Wylie asked.

"We're not sure. We don't know how long it maintains your ability to heal instantaneously. My guess would be to take it every six hours while in combat, just to be safe."

"Roger that."

"This group runs a legit casino in Illinois. Chicago was the perfect place because of its location. Do a bit of Recon first, obviously. It's the Americano High Rise Casino."

"What about civilians? Collateral damage?"

"Save as many as you can. Tear gas each floor until they vacate. The cartel will stay to protect their property. You can snipe them if they egress, or go in and annihilate. Your call."

"Copy that."

"As far as we can tell, there're about fifty men you'll take care of. Surveille for an exact count."

"Roger that, sir."

General Hawkins paused. "You have the termination sensor in your head. You know how to use it, I assume."

"I do, sir. When I'm on a mission where I can be terminated, I'm to activate the frequency so if my organs stop for five minutes, I'll explode to protect the science behind my existence." Wylie paused, then added, "but the Charge makes the term frequency unnecessary, sir."

"Correct. But on any mission, invoke the termination frequency. Each time, no exception. Say you didn't have Yellow Charge in your system... you forgot to take it, or ran out... and you get killed. You'll die then explode if you've activated the frequency... unless you're incinerated by those bullets before it can detonate. We, uh, *do* have to protect the science behind your creation. We can't let it fall into the wrong hands."

"Understood, sir."

"You leave tomorrow. I'll have the captain take you to the weapons bunker and let you lose." He turned in the direction of the door.

"We're good to go."

Wylie was escorted to the weapon bunker by Captain Abara to prepare for his mission.

"Place your eye against the retina scanner, Wylie," the leader instructed. "No one gets in here without the general's express permission."

A set of dense metal doors opened into a second smaller room. They walked forward to another set of massive barriers.

"Palm scanner," the captain instructed.

Both men scanned their palms and the second set of doors slid open to reveal an enormous stockpile. Rows of handguns, shotguns, rifles, and grenade launchers hung on pegs in the walls. There were knives and other equipment by the box loads.

Wylie's internal scanner clicked on and fed him information about each item. As he reached for an M-16 a large man with a bronze complexion appeared. His scanner instantly assessed the man's proximity and details about his large frame.

The captain said, "Hello, Nigel! This is Wylie, Special Ops, and he requires the best of the best. Can you please advise him?"

Nigel Thomas had an avid fascination for weaponry. He was a consultant for the Army who tested and improved weapons before they were manufactured on a large scale.

Nigel was proud of his cache. It was the largest newly manufactured military weapon collection in the world.

"Yes, of course, Captain Abara." He said with a deep timbre. He said to Wylie. "You came to the right place. What's your flavor?"

"I want top notch." Wylie said as his eyes scanned the room. "I'll need a grenade launcher, tear gas, throwing knives, a handgun, an assault rifle, and a shitload of ammo."

Nigel's eyes widened. "You going on a suicide mission, son? Where's the rest of your team?"

Abara spoke up, "No details, Nigel. Just give the man what he needs."

Nigel studied the captain before walking to a large case holding knives. He held his hand to the glass. The material glowed before disappearing.

The man took out a wicked dagger with three blades twisting to the hilt. "This is a weapon that I based on the Jagdkommando, the Austrian Armed Special Forces knife. I've adapted it for field use." Nigel said and handed it to Wylie.

"Eight inches of titanium with rubberized grip, hollowed handle for light weight, and twisting tri blades sharpened with micro-technology," Wylie said as he absorbed his internal feed.

Nigel's eyes widened. "Er... yes. I've put a special wash on the blades that sharpens them with every use. Each time it's used, it becomes more lethal."

Wylie nodded. "A self-sharpening knife used to kill. I'll take it."

Nigel appraised the younger man with interest. "Here's another self-sharpener." Nigel handed Wylie a smaller knife. "This one I've adapted from the Karambit."

"The Indonesian knife whose design was based on a tiger's claw."

"Right. I'm impressed. We should get together and talk weapons, my boy," Nigel exclaimed. His eyes brightened, "Yes, I've modified and Americanized this blade as well."

Wylie took the knife and held it by the circle finger hold. "Six point five inches total length. Three-inch curved alloy blade, self-sharpening glaze, single-edged flat grind, three point five centimeters thick, black wash."

"Where did you learn so much?" Nigel asked. "A man after my own heart." Nigel placed a big hand on his chest and staggered a step. He grinned as he looked at Wylie.

Abara rolled his eyes.

"Do you want more knives?" Nigel asked.

Wylie nodded. "Yes, I want to strap a few here and there."

"Come. Choose from these." Nigel waved his hand across layers of self-sharpening knives.

Wylie chose a Glock, a few Bowies of varying lengths, several varieties of KA-Bars, and three smaller switchblades. Nigel guided them to another section.

"Handguns... nine-millimeter or forty-five cal?" Nigel asked.

"One of each," Wylie said.

Nigel handed Wylie a Glock 19 and M1911.

"These are good guns," Wylie said after palming them, "But let me see a Glock 22 and a M9 Beretta."

"Good choices, son," Nigel approved. He switched the guns. "You've got a lot of power with the Glock's clip. Fifteen rounds of forty cals. Then you've got the light weight and versatility with the Beretta's nine-millimeter."

Wylie added the guns to his growing pile. "Assault rifles?"

The big man turned to another wall filled with guns. "This way." He took a rifle off the wall. "This is a modified M4," he said.

Wylie strapped it on. He said, "It's lighter than normal."

"Yes, and carries more ammo," Nigel said. "It's got a bump stock for recoil. 1500 rounds a minute."

The captain whistled. "Normal M4s only fire 900."

"Yes," Nigel said. "Accurate to six-hundred meters. This bad boy can hit a fly nine hundred meters away."

Wylie put it on the pile.

"And now for the grenade launcher. I've got an improved M203. It can fit under the M16 with accuracy of one-thousand meters."

"Gimme."

"Anything else, soldier?" Nigel asked. "Night vision goggles? Thermal imaging equipment?"

"He's got that already," Captain Abara said.

"Not like mine."

"Believe me. His is better," the captain said.

Nigel raised his brows, and his lips parted slightly. His face read: *Who are you cheating on me with?*

"Besides tear gas, grenades, and ammo, I'm all set," Wylie said looking at his pile.

"No armor? Vests?"

Wylie shook his head.

"Okay, man. It's your life," Nigel said. He was still shaking his head as he led them into another room where boxes of ammo lay in wait. "Regular ammo here. The speciality stuff is in the back."

Wylie interrupted. "Forget the regular stuff. I want Electro Rounds."

"How did you..."

"The general told me what I'll be facing."

Nigel's face went white and he muttered, "Impossible."

The captain's grim expression told the weapon's master they weren't joking.

"You're... going up against my invention?" Nigel asked. He swallowed. "How many have this?" He fisted the ammo before handing the missile-like bullet to Wylie.

The captain reminded him. "Nigel, remember? No questions."

"But... he's going on a death mission," Nigel said. "These bullets have incredible kill power. You don't even have to hit your target in a strike zone. All you have to do is scratch them with one of these, any place on their body, and it's lights out. Hell, even the breeze passing by could activate the reaction." The technologist ran his hand through his hair.

Wylie lifted the bullet and looked it over before handing it back. To all appearances, it looked like a normal cartridge. However, internally, Wylie could see the shell contained a cylinder of liquid fire that would combust on any living target.

"What liquid do you use in the chamber?" Wylie asked.

"How... do you know?" Nigel asked. "There's no way you could know that."

"I can see it."

Nigel studied the round. "You have better eyes than I do, son," he said. "I can't tell a damn lick of difference."

Wylie said nothing while the big man scratched his head. He offered no explanation.

"Oh, I'll also require flash bangs and possibly... well, anything that is safe to help civilians want to vacate quickly. Tear gas is pretty harsh..."

"I have just the thing," Nigel said. He walked to a container full of hexagonal items. "These are Stench Bombs. It's a similar formula to tear gas but it doesn't affect vision... unless they don't vacate in fifteen minutes. The smell increases until all senses are impaired. It takes twenty to twenty-five minutes to reach full capacity, most will choose to leave in the first ten. It's much more effective for encouraging an exodus."

"Can they be deployed by the M203?"

"Definitely. You may want a gas mask if you use these," Nigel suggested. "And if your enemy doesn't have them, it'll be easy breezy."

Wylie was unsure if his senses would be immune, so he added a gas mask to his stash.

"Oh, there *is* one more thing," Wylie said.

"Yes?"

"I need enough power to take down a building."

Nigel pursed his lips and gave a long, low whistle. He opened his mouth to ask more questions but shut it with a glare from the captain.

"Sure, son. Ask, and you shall receive."

He led Wylie over to another room. There were a variety of plastic explosives and bombs of all sizes. He went directly to a case filled with small chip-like devices.

"There are ten explosives in this box," Nigel said, placing a small plastic case into Wylie's palm. "Take a block of plastic-adhesive clay to secure the bomb, then stick one of these little dudes in, and viola."

"How much time will I have to place and retreat?" Wylie asked.

"No worries. They're chipped technology. You add a frequency control to detonate after they're in place. They'll detonate from a half mile away."

"Awesome." Wylie took the needed incendiaries.

Nigel said, "You sure you're going alone, son? You'll need a few guys to help you carry all that."

The Captain laughed. "He'll manage."

Wylie stared through his scope, a man on a mission.

Come nightfall, most of the clientele will be at the casino, ready to party The best strike time would be right before the place fills. If I wait, many will be impaired from adrenaline or alcohol. If I can time it right, the civilians will leave and those who remain will be the targets...

He watched the business for nearly the entire day. The casino was encased in glass and rested on a motorized platform that slowly turned so all gamers could eventually have a spectacular view of the city. A restaurant and a stage were in the middle of the casino flanked by a wrap-a-round bar. The extravagant loft stood over eight stories of hotel rooms.

Precisely at four-thirty in the afternoon, Wylie took his 203 launcher loaded with a Stench Bomb. No one was in the casino area yet, so he aimed at the most centralized location, the grill, and fired.

The bomb spiraled through the thick glass, but the huge pane didn't shatter. It simply punched a fist-sized hole and detonated in the grill.

Slowly, a mist expelled. Within minutes, doors above the gaming arena began to open. Men emerged onto the balcony overlooking the floors. They leaned over the railing, studying the scene. Most held a hand over their nose and mouth.

Wylie fitted a second Stench Bomb into the M203 and waited. He watched the men become more and more active in the high rise. He could practically hear their panic and confusion as they scrambled looking for the cause of their increasingly impaired senses. Quickly, they assessed the stench to be a threat and retrieved guns.

Within ten minutes, men were covering their orifices with anything they could secure, and in fifteen, many were retching. They finally made a beeline for the elevators and stairs.

Wylie waited a few minutes more and fired the second Stench Bomb into the seventh-floor hallway, two levels beneath the casino. Already customers on the eighth floor were crowding into stairwells. No time for the slow elevators.

Thirty minutes later, people flooded out of every exit, holding their mouths, and many vomited once outside.

Wylie smiled. He'd vacated the entire high rise with three stench bombs. He put the launcher aside and checked his other weaponry. The pistols were strapped to his waist band. Knives were fastened in a variety of places: ankle, waist, under his arm, and to his thighs. Clips hung from many loops on his vest, and the M4 was in his hand with the strap slung from his shoulder across his body. The gas mask hung limply around his neck.

Wylie walked toward the building. As he approached, he unzipped a pouch on his hip, took out a yellow capsule, and popped it in his mouth.

His readout indicated forty-six people were still on sight. It was in the ballpark of what the general anticipated. Wylie activated Chameleon and was ready for business.

A group of twenty-five men stood far enough away from the building to protect their senses. They were animated and spoke in rapid Spanish. Wylie stalked closer to listen before opening fire.

"What in the hell is going on?" a man asked.

"I do not know," another responded. He gestured wildly, and his eyes bulged with excitement. "We were in the offices, and suddenly we heard a little noise, like a pop, but no alarms went off. Shortly after, the stench started, and we couldn't stay."

"Where are the gas masks?" a third asked.

"Geraldo will be back soon," said the man that appeared to be the most in-charge of the group. "He and Enrique just left to get the rest. We only had twenty or so inside... we never thought we'd use them."

"Yes, they are inside trying to see what is going on and who is attacking us," another person said. "The attackers... they'll be sorry. They must not know they are messing with the Sinaloa Cartel."

Isaac offered a rough laugh and said, "They will find out shortly."

"I almost can't take the smell from here!" the first guy said. "What in the hell is that reek?"

"Did you shit your pants, Juan?" teased another.

"Shut the fuck up, Ricardo."

"Knock it off, you two," the leader snapped. "We've got enough trouble as it is. We don't need more with you starting in." He paused, then said, "*Dammit!* We have a big shipment going out today. We can't load under these circumstances! Miguel will be *pissed*!"

Those words quieted the crowd. No one moved for a few moments.

"That's too bad," said Wylie in English.

The men's faces took a few moments to register the fact that someone other than their group had spoken. They looked at each other with brows raised and began craning their necks. Some shuffled about in their gathering.

"Who said that?" Ricardo asked, pulling out a pistol. Most had pistols and assault rifles already in-hand.

"Your worst nightmare," Wylie answered, again in English.

The members of the cartel saw a man materialize in their midst holding military-issued pistols in each hand. His arms were extended, and he opened fire directly after appearing. Men began exploding into ash within moments.

The men further away tried to run and take cover while returning fire. The assassin holstered one of his weapons and held up a hand. The projectile of the bullets instantly changed direction. Ones making a direct line shot upwards while others to either side pinged in new directions. No bullet could penetrate the invisible shield emanating from his hand.

The outsider aimed his second pistol and pressed the trigger. The Electro Rounds found their targets. Fine, gray mist rained around him. The devil's silhouette stepped toward the casino as the smoky remains cleared.

Wylie smiled. *Now that was fun.* Hesecured the gas mask and entered the building.

No threats on the main level. Wylie's visual scanner read most of the targets were in the stairwells. He saw their red-energy signatures moving up the building's skeleton. He followed his prey like a fox stalking a mouse.

Minutes later, Wylie could see three men in front of him, so he pulled out his Beretta. As he closed in, he heard muffled breathing through face masks.

The man in front slowed, then stopped. He turned in the dimly lit stairwell to face the other two.

"Do you hear that?" he asked.

The two who followed stopped to listen. "Uh, yes. It sounds like a man is standing just behind us with a mask on... but no one's there." He pointed even though all could clearly see.

The second man looked at the first's finger which seemed to hang in the air in a smoky silhouette before falling to the floor in a cloud of ash. A second blast rocketed from the stairwell just under him, but the man didn't have time to register what was happening before he was hit. The third man was able to fire one round in his general direction but seconds later, his gun clattered to the floor and somersaulted through gray smoke down several flights of stairs.

Wylie proceeded. On the seventh floor, he found two men in the hall where he'd embedded the second Stench Bomb. One was holding up the empty cartridge.

The middle-aged man said, "Look. Someone is trying to compromise our business." He dangled the empty shell from his hand so the other could see.

"What is that? It looks like a grenade... kind of. Is it safe?"

"It is empty now, genius, so it's safe enough. The damn stuff wasn't harmless when we all ran out of the building, though."

"Maybe you shouldn't touch it," Genius said. "Who knows what kind of chemicals were in it."

"It's too late now. Let's take it to Miguel. His scientists can take a look." said the other.

"You don't have to bother because I can tell you," Wylie said. They turned to see him leaning against the wall with his leg propped up. "It's a Stench Bomb, and I put it there."

He smiled and shot them at close range . They exploded and covered the hall in a layer of ash.

Literally, I was made for this. This is fucking fun.

Wylie scanned the floors above him and detected eleven signatures. He eagerly took the stairs two at a time. When he entered the casino, he saw five men gathered around the grill and two inspecting the hole in the window. The other four patrolled the area.

"The dipshits shot a fucking grenade into the grill," said the man stooped over the appliance, peering at the hexagon wedged between the metal. Although the mask distorted his words, he was clearly understood.

"A grenade? That ain't no grenade, Amigo. Well," Green Shirt shrugged. "I'll never eat here again. I mean, who wants food that smells like shit?"

"We'll have to get a new grill, obviously," said Amigo.

"And have some guys clean this place up. It'll take months to get the smell outta here," Green Shirt said, his voice muffled. He kicked some debris in disgust.

"Miguel's gonna be pissed," Amigo said. "I'd hate to see his reaction, and he should be here any time."

Green Shirt nodded. After a pause, he asked, "You think the air's clear yet? I hate these things." He pointed to the bulky mask.

Amigo said, "Be my guest and see."

Green Shirt laughed. "Oh, no, Amigo. I don't want to know that badly."

Wylie angled behind Green Shirt. With a switchblade, he cut the straps of the gas mask. It clattered to the floor.

Green Shirt started coughing but was able to speak.

"What the FUCK just happened?" he asked between coughs.

"You klutz! You knocked your mask off," Amigo said.

Just then, his mask also clanked on the floor. The other three stared at it. Within seconds, all masks joined the first two on the tile.

A guard said. "Man, these straps were cut."

"I need to use my inhaler," the fifth man gasped, "But I'm afraid to breathe in. I need my mask!" He held the protection to his face.

Amigo said. "We've been infiltrated!"

The five men pulled their weapons and faced outwards, their backs to each other.

One of the men on patrol came into view. Wylie shot him and the two hunkering down by the window. He was still invisible.

"You dumbass! You just took out three of our men!" Amigo cried.

Dumbass yelled back, "I didn't fire!"

"Their ash is all over! If you didn't fire, who did?"

No one answered. After the pops of weapon fire, the other three men ran in, weapons drawn. They were poofs of dust suspended in the air as soon as they were in range.

"Mother fuckersstop fuckin' shooting our men, Dumb asses!" Amigo screamed.

"WE AREN'T SHOOTING!" the four shouted.

Green Shirt said in as calm of a voice as he could manage, "Amigo, we aren't firing. It sounds like we are, but no one has. None of our weapons have been discharged."

Amigo looked everywhere. "What the fuck is going on?" He spoke rapidly as sweat popped out on his forehead. "Those men didn't just mist on their own."

Wylie appeared on their left.

"Who is that?" Extra Guard Man asked. The group followed his gaze while swinging weapons in the general direction.

Wylie let them catch a glimpse, but he disappeared before they could get a bead on him. Next, he appeared behind them.

"There he is!" yelled Green Shirt.

Again, Wylie disappeared.

"It's a fucking predator!" said Amigo, pointing. "Like in a movie!"

"Shit, he's right!" Dumbass said.

Asthma was breathing hard. He pressed his gas mask harder on his face.

"Are you shitting me? An asthma attack now?" Amigo said. "When we need you the most?" He kicked at him, none-too-gently.

Wylie materialized, Glock 22 in hand.

The asthmatic man dropped his gun and fell to the floor, clutching his mask to his face as if it would fix a gunshot wound to his chest.

"Time's up," Wylie said with a smile. "Your compadres are nearly here. Miguel, is it? He's coming up the stairwell now with fourteen more men."

The group of four acted with synchronized movements. Wylie held up his hand to deflect incoming bullets then returned fire. Ash rained on the man gasping on the floor. Wylie took out his Jagdkommandoknife. It glinted evilly as light ran down the twisting length. When Wylie leaned over the writhing man who tried to talk.

The man coughed, then stuttered a terrified, "Noooo."

"Yes," Wylie said with a smile. He pushed the man's shoulder until he lay flat on his back. Without hesitation, he plunged the deadly blade into the man's heart. A geyser of blood bubbled from the jagged hole in his chest.

Wylie stared in fascination at the crimson flood. His hands, of their own accord, reached down and touched it. Wylie was whisked to another time, another life.

Five years earlier:

Wylie looked at his blood-covered hands and grinned. *That'll show the bastards.* His intense anger turned to artistic joy and then to an indescribable hunger. *No one would ever understand what the sweet taste of revenge was like. Oh, how they would pay.*

122

Once more, Wylie looked at his hands. *Damn that was fun.* He touched the blood covering them. *Funny, but didn't his fingers look a bit shorter? And where did the light dusting of freckles come from? Maybe it was debris that got stuck in the congealing blood.*

Wylie froze when he realized that although the room looked familiar, it was no longer where he'd been a few seconds ago. He was no longer on a mission against the drug cartel in a hotel casino, but he was at a lavishly furnished home that appeared to be hosting a dinner party. Except... the host was the dinner. Wylie stood quickly from his crouched position.

What is going on?

He approached a mirror and peered at his reflection. He was covered from head to toe with splattered blood. His mouth was stained with it, and even his teeth appeared pinkish. That was a bit shocking, but even more disturbing was the face looking back. It was not Wylie's. A short, thin man stared back, sandy hair not Wylie's rich brown. And blue eyes, not brown.

Wylie sat, feeling dazed.

"Wright." he said.

He knew that man was *Wright*.

Back to the second mission:

Wylie was brought back to the present by a cold barrel of a gun pressed against his temple. Six men stood protectively around the leader, the remaining henchmen further back, not overly attentive.

"Look who finally is here," Miguel said with a smirk. He tapped his head then continued, "You are a one-man army, No?" He pressed the gun with more force into Wylie's skull. "Who sent you?"

Wylie's eyes narrowed, but he said nothing.

"You dare to defy me?" Miguel said. His voice moved from quiet intensity to escalating aggression. He pressed the gun even harder. "While I hold a gun to your head? I'd say you weren't very smart, but you must have some intelligence to get as far as you have."

He waited for a response. When none came, Miguel growled.

"No? It's a shame you came all this way... just to die."

Miguel pulled the trigger. Wylie was aware of a moment-by-moment account of the bullet's progress. First, the tip of the bullet forced its way into his skin. He could feel the liquid dispense that would incinerate his body, but the Yellow Charge was already at work. It encased the injection in a force field and reversed the direction. As the bullet pushed its way back out of his skin, it repaired all damage. The bullet fell uselessly to the floor, and the liquid evaporated once it hit the air.

Wylie launched to his feet. Miguel was stunned, immobilized. Wylie was as a tiger,his lethal claw, the Karambit, held deftly, and he swiped upward with deadly force. It cut across the man's jugular before his opponent could make a defensive move.

Miguel fell. Wylie spun and threw a smaller Bowie knife into the next man's temple. His eyes went wide as blood sprayed from his head. His body thumped alongside his boss. Again, the Karambit's deadly bite was already deeply embedded in the next man's neck. Wylie jabbed and slashed through the remaining men, obliterating them with the scythe-like blade of the Karambit and the lethal punch of the Jagdkommando.

Seven men lay with unseeing eyes, spilling liters of blood onto the flooring, while the rest ran for the exits. Wylie grinned. He lifted the M4 and fifteen-hundred rounds of bullets a minute shredded their bodies.

No reason to waste the Electro Rounds. That should do it. The rifle rested against his chest supported by a strap. He didn't notice the muzzle's heat as it burned into his chest. Immediately, his skin repaired itself.

Wylie ran a final scan of the building, there were three additional signatures on the fifth floor. After wiping out the final targets, he would burn the building to the ground,finishing the job with flourish.

With his pistols drawn, Wylie arrived on the fifth floor. Three people were passed out. A woman lay in her vomit with a child clutched in her arms Another unconscious young child was nearby. Wylie scoffed, and holstered his weapons.

These ones don't deserve to die. Just bystanders. He sighed, then hoisted the woman over his shoulder. Her wet hair slapped against his back. He managed to scoop a child under each arm and make it out of the building. Once a safe distance away, he gently placed them on the ground and went back to complete his mission.

Wylie reentered the building and placed the tiny plastique explosives in eight locations around the base of the building. When finished, he stood a safe distance away, still close enough to detonate the charges. A small, hand-held device emitted a high-pitched frequency which set off the bombs in a deadly chain reaction.

Wylie watched as the building collapsed on itself. A mushroom cloud of dust boiled into the air until all that was left of the fancy casino was a mountain of rubble. The gambling hotel was now as functional as the Sinaloa Cartel in Chicago.

AFTER MISSION TWO: Wylie

Wylie relaxed back onto his military-issued cot. It wasn't much as far as comfort was concerned, but that wasn't his first priority. He needed time to think.

His eyes wandered about his makeshift room on the base. Wylie was still earning his experimenters' trust. After a probationary period of ninety days, they would allow him to live either with men in the barracks or on his own in the community.

Wylie's thoughts returned to the recently completed mission. *So, what happened today? It was not okay to be in the middle of a mission and freeze. I let a memory of some kind whisk me away. If it hadn't been for the Yellow Charge, I'd have been dead.*

But where did the memory come from? Who am I, anyway? Before the mission, I'd only been a machine who cared about mission orders with no thoughts of my own, but after my first kill, I processed information more personally. Now, I have other thoughts not related to my job. That isn't normal, is it?

The thing which bothered him the most, though, was the man in the mirror. *Who was Wright?*

Wylie sat up, straightening his spine, and relaxed his extremities. He deepened his breathing and entered a meditative trance. He used the data accesses programmed in his mind to research any person named Wright. Data revealed a newspaper article about a man by that name who was convicted of murder and recently executed; and another memory.

TWO YEARS AGO: Private Inmate Meeting Room

"Can I ask you something, Doc?" Wright said through gritted teeth.

They sat in the interrogation room at the metal table with plexiglass and bars on the windows.

"Of course." Dr. Turner stopped scribbling and leaned back in his anchored chair across. He met his client's eyes.

"Why me?" Wright asked. "You could choose any inmate down here, and most would jump at the chance to be reborn and kill for the government. Why me? I didn't want this, yet I got it. No choice involved. It pisses me off to no end."

"Because your love for killing is perfect. Your drive is more… innate than in the other men."

"I told you I didn't want my story in a damn book, so instead, you're going to make me relive it over and over again?" Wright shifted and his chains rattled. "That's cruel and unusual punishment, Doc."

"We need to combine a love for killing with the mind of a soldier. The two should complement the other. If it's any consolation, your life will be different than it is now."

"I don't see how you can say that," Wright said. "Killing is killing, isn't it? You want a man painting your little government scenes with body mutilation?"

"I doubt that will occur again, Wright."

"Don't be too sure. I'm pretty damn hard headed. Unless you can be sure, you need to reconsider me for your little experiment. I don't want to be a part of this, and I hold grudges."

"So you've said." Dr. Turner shrugged and went back to his legal pad.

Wright sucked in air through flared nostrils. "You got any kids, Doc?"

Dr. Turner looked up from his notes. "Yes. I have one."

"A daughter."

"Where are you going with this, Wright?" He paused and crossed his top leg over the other and jiggled his foot. "I don't tolerate threats."

"You'll be more than tolerating if you bring me back, Doc," Wright said, slamming a fist on the metal table. "I'm trying to warn you. You'll be living it. You *and* your daughter will pay for this."

"Wright. If you want to keep your mind and not get drugged, stop acting like an animal. You may be caged, but you have a brain. Use it." The features on his were rigid and determined.

Wright watched the doctor stand and buzz for the guards.

AFTER MISSION TWO: Wylie's Return from the Memory

Wylie came back into awareness with a new understanding. Anger towards the doctor radiated through him, and remnants of a memory.

Things are, indeed, different now, just like Doc promised. I have control of myself during killings. As a soldier, I carry out a mission, so my angry passion is gone, but I feel it rising in my soul. I suddenly need to find out more about the good doctor and his daughter. A promise is a promise, after all.

PRESENT DAY: Detectives Jewels and Joe

Jewels and Joe were buzzed into The Disease Center. They walked through the double-paned doors and found themselves in a small waiting room. Six navy chairs lined the wall and were affixed to the floor alongside a few small white tables. A camera from every angle focused on any who visited this secured area. There was a second locked door that led beyond the waiting room.

Two women behind sliding plexiglass windows looked at the couple expectantly. Joe sat in one of the chairs while Jewels approached the window.

"We need to speak with anyone who worked closely with Dr. Muller, please," Jewels said, sliding her credentials into the opening under the plexiglass.

"One moment, please," said a woman as she looked over the badge's details.

Jewels retrieved her ID and took a seat by Joe. Several minutes ticked by before the second door finally swung open. A thin woman with graying frizzy hair stepped into the waiting room. She had attempted to tame her mane by parting it and smothering it with product.

"Detectives Combs and Polten. Will you please follow me?" Her voice was deep, melodic, and all business.

The detectives followed the middle-aged woman into a narrow office and took the two seats on the opposite side of her desk.

"I'm Doctor Marla Taylor, head of research. How may I help you?"

Joe shook her hand, and Jewels followed suit.

"We're on the 'Eat Your Heart Out Killer' case," Joe informed her. "As you may know, Dr. Muller was his second victim. We need to find out what we can about the good doctor so we can stop this killer from striking again. There's a connection here somewhere."

"I understand," Dr. Taylor agreed. "I can tell you Dr. Muller's job was to study various pathologies to determine auto-immune thresholds."

Jewel's mouth opened a little before she recovered. She asked, "Are you saying his practice was to see how ill someone could get and still function, or to see how long a body could live with it before passing on?"

"Both," Dr. Taylor pushed an escaped tendril of hair away from her face. "When someone becomes afflicted with one of our studied pathogens, Dr. Muller's job was to observe and note any changes. Of course, treatment and patient response to therapy was also recorded."

The doctor must have interpreted Jewel's mortification, because she added, "The only way we can find cures to different contaminants are to study the symptoms and how the diseases function. We must try different strategies and study their effects to determine what will work. All our participants have exhausted other avenues. This place," she waved a hand, "is their last chance."

"What do you do with this research?" Joe's face was devoid of emotion. Jewels knew he was masking his disapproval.

Dr. Taylor met his leveled stare. "We use this data to develop cures, of course. Cures don't happen overnight. It takes years to discover what can effectively destroy a pathogen and not harm its host."

"Does anyone else have access to this data?" he asked.

Dr. Taylor leaned back in her chair and contemplated. She finally answered, "That data goes into classified military folders for their use."

"Interesting," Jewels said. "I didn't realize the Army was into using private companies to further their research."

"I didn't say this was a partnership with the government," the doctor said. "They are merely interested in what we find out."

"Interesting," Jewels said, her brows arched.

"Is this standard practice for the military?" Joe asked.

"I really couldn't say," Dr. Taylor responded. "I would guess that it is. It's no secret there has been biological warfare development worldwide. Why wouldn't the military want to study what we find here? I'm sure there's been pathogen-weaponry development, so there's even more need for cures or for vaccines for deployed soldiers."

Joe leaned forward and said, "Yes, that's true. But were you aware the military was also involved with the last person we interviewed?"

"Really?" the doctor said, "Another victim?"

"Possibly," Jewels said with a shrug.

"Is there anything else noteworthy Dr. Muller researched?" Joe pressed. His sternness subsided a bit. He didn't want to discourage the doctor from divulging more information.

"No," Dr. Taylor said, "basically, he studied diseases, how long they incubated, what their effects were, how they responded to various treatments, and how long the disease lasted until the subject terminated."

Jewels asked, "Do you have any connections with Technology of Tomorrow?"

Her face tightened momentarily, and a small tic formed at the edge of her mouth.

"Um," Dr. Taylor replied, "I haven't, but I'm uncertain about Dr. Muller. He may have."

"How long have you been on this project, Dr. Taylor?" Jewels asked.

"About three months."

Jewels nodded.

"Do you know if any of his patients tried to heal themselves with cryogenics?" Joe asked.

"Or did he use any substances supplied by Technology of Tomorrow in his procedures?" Jewels pressed.

"Again, I'm unsure. I can ask around and find out." Dr. Taylor stood and looked through a few papers.

Jewels's eyes met Joe's. Each held the other's look of concern at the doctor's dismissive body language.

"Anything you can do to add to our compilation of data can only help," Joe added.

Doctor Taylor said with clipped words, "I'll do my best." She glanced at them but continued to rummage around on the desk.

"Look," Jewels said, as she stood. She touched Dr. Taylor briefly on the arm. "We'd really appreciate any help you can give us. We're uncovering some concerning things, things that may help us stop a serial murderer. Since you've been here three months, you're probably still overwhelmed with all your responsibilities. Please, give us a call if you find anything in your learning curve that could help us stop this man. He's brutal and *extremely* dangerous."

Dr. Taylor's eyes widened, and she stopped rifling through her papers.

"Are you saying... I could be in danger?" Her voice was softer.

Joe said, "We can't rule it out. You can only help us save lives, doctor."

"And that's what your whole professional life is all about, isn't it?" Jewels said. "That's what ours is about, too. Help us save lives."

Dr. Taylor sat down. She let out a pent-up breath and gave a small nod.

"I'm not saying anything officially," she said.

"Off the record, then?" Joe asked.

Dr. Taylor gave another small nod. "I – I don't know much."

"Anything can help," Joe said.

Jewels added, "Possibly more than you know."

"I've found just a hint of possible involvement," Dr. Taylor said. "They were working on something big, but there's not much in the notes about what, precisely. It's like someone came in and took a good portion of the research."

"Research on?"

"Finding cures," she said. "I think they found a big one."

"A big... cure?" Joe asked. His eyes widened in genuine surprise.

Dr. Taylor nodded. "Yes. Clients were coming in with advanced stages of infections. Stage four cancer where their internal systems were chuck full, hearts with 99% blockage with advanced stages of congestive heart failure. Diabetic people with gangrenous extremities and glaucoma. We even had a few nearly terminal cases

135

of influenza and COVID-19. I could go on. After Dr. Muller and Dr. Torrent got together, these people walked away with one-hundred percent recovery rates. Tell me they weren't on to something. However, I don't know what, and that's the truth."

"Who's 'they'?" Jewels asked.

"I - I'm not sure. Dr. Torrent was involved, I think, and of course, Dr. Muller."

She stood slowly and walked to her office door, indicating their time was at an end.

"Look, I can't tell you more than that, and I'm already nervous about what I've divulged."

"Thank you so much for your trust," Joe said.

Jewels nodded her agreement with a smile. "Yes. I can't tell you how much we appreciate it."

Each detective shook the doctor's hand.

"Thank you, too," Dr. Taylor said. "I hope I've helped."

"You have." Jewels promised. She laid her card on her desk. "If anything further comes up please reach out."

After the detectives took their leave, Dr. Taylor sat down. Her hands shook slightly as she put the card in the top desk drawer.

"What have I gotten myself into?" she whispered.

THREE AND A HALF MONTHS PRIOR: Dr. Marla Taylor

Dr. Marla Taylor sat nervously in the waiting room of Dr. Fritz Muller. She smoothed her burgundy skirt and then patted her hair. She hoped the hair product was still winning the war against her frizz.

Finally, an office door opened and a woman in a crisp blue pencil skirt suit stepped out, escorted by a forty-something year-old man.

The man said, "Thank you so much, Dr. Borenstein. It was nice visiting with you."

"I'll expect a call," she said with a teasing smile.

Did Marla imagine a bit of a flirtatious eye flutter from the woman?

"We'll call or email when we make our decision," Dr. Muller offered. They shook hands. The woman's face hardened a bit when she saw Marla waiting for the next interview slot.

Good morning, Dr. Taylor," he greeted. "I appreciate your punctuality. Won't you come into my office?"

She gave a smile as she passed by him.

"My apologies for the small office." He said from his messy desk. We spend our money on research and possible cures rather than comfort. In addition, we don't spend a lot of time in our headquarters."

"I understand," she said.

The chair creaked under Dr. Muller's weight. He leaned back and studied her. His intense stare bored into her soul.

"Tell me about yourself," he said.

"I'm Dr. Marla Taylor," she began. "I've been a pathologist for nineteen and a half years." She nervously cleared her throat. "I've only worked in a clinical setting. I specialize in new treatment protocols for known pathogens. My treatment modalities have a 98% effectiveness rate."

Dr. Muller leafed through her file. He stopped on a printed email.

"I'd say you're underselling yourself," he said with a smile. "You're highly praised and come with superb recommendations. Tell me, why do you want to leave a job you're obviously so successful at?" Those eyes kept up the focused stare. It was unnerving.

Marla cleared her throat. "I am passionate about finding cures, but I don't care to be in a stationary position the rest of my life. Although labs will forever be a part of my professional life, I don't care to be in one forever. I want more. For my own personal satisfaction."

The doctor laced his fingers to form a steeple, and pressed them against his lips.

"I assume you know what you'd be getting into if you come to work for us."

"Yes. I'll be in a lab some, but my job would be to help oversee terminal patients inflicted with different microorganisms. I would record symptoms, prescribe treatments, and watch the effects of my recommendations on their healing... or decline. I also realize in a facility like this, I'll be working with more of the extreme situations… ones I'm not used to seeing."

"Yes. A woman with your knowledge base would be very valued in this facility."

"I would be happy to be a part of it," she said with a smile.

"Tell me a little about your personal life. What do you do for stress management?"

Dr. Taylor smiled. "I have a grown son who just got married. He's moved to another state. I'm unmarried because my marriage is to my work. Yes, I do know that I need breaks to refresh my mind, but that is usually time spent reading before bed or watching a few television shows."

Dr. Muller said, "Very good. It's not every day we run across someone with your qualifications. We'd be happy to have you aboard." Dr. Muller said. "You'll be a probationary hire. Then, if we like what we see, you'd be directly under me as Head of the Department."

Marla's expression brightened. "I couldn't ask for more."

"Don't you want to hear about your pay?" Dr. Muller asked with a smile. "I hope it will make you even happier." He told her a surprising amount, and she nodded gleefully.

"To start, you'll have a case load I'll compile. You'll collect data with the help of some aides. You'll write down everything: what you prescribe, the effects, and so on and so forth."

"Yes, I'm happy to do all that."

"You do realize that you'll see death here. In a lab, you weren't exposed to actually seeing it. I just want you to be aware. It can be quite... disturbing."

"I want to make a difference, Dr. Muller. I want to help the world heal as much as I can. If doing this makes me uncomfortable, then that makes the satisfaction even deeper. To truly help is not what makes one comfortable. I jump at the opportunity. Thank you so very much."

"Welcome aboard, Dr. Taylor. You can start next week, or just as soon as you can wrap things up at your other place of employment."

Each stood and shook hands on the finalized deal.

"I'm happy to be here. Thank you again, Dr. Muller. You won't regret this."

"I'll prepare your contract. Stop by in a few days to sign it, please."

"Oh yes, I can't wait."

When Marla left the building, she was giddy. She practically floated to her car. She was finally going to get to help society in a way that she felt was the most beneficial use of her skill set.

As she put the key in the ignition, Marla wondered vaguely about how the other candidate would take this news.

PRESENT DAY – Dr. Mathew Turner

Dr. Turner stared out his window into the black of night. His eyes were open, but he did not see.

Not much matters anymore, he thought.

All the things he strived to accomplish were valueless now. Yes, he had money. Yes, he was respected. Yes, he'd be immortal in the pages of research journals. His name would live perpetually, but he no longer cared.

What was life if you had no one to live for? He wondered. *The only person I ever loved is gone, and it's all my fault. I never knew how much she really mattered to me. Why hadn't I listened to her? Why? Because I know best, goddamn it.* He slammed his fist into his palm.

He knew everything, or thought he did, and that's why his daughter had died a terrible death. *Oh, how Wylie must be laughing.*

Do I still call him Wylie? Or Wright? Does it really matter? Whatever his name, he has an agenda. And that plan involves taking out all of us who experimented on him. It's just a matter of time, thought Mathew Turner, *before he comes for me.*

Mathew fished in his pocket for his cell. He punched in the number for the General.

"Colonel Landers."

"Colonel Landers, this is Priority Code 7 Bravo Delta 5."

"One moment while I dispatch to the general."

The General's disciplined voice filled the line. "Yes?"

"It's Matt."

"Yes."

"Hey, I was, um, wondering if you were aware about Wylie."

The general didn't respond.

"He… he killed my daughter, sir."

"I'm sorry."

Matt was unable to speak for a few moments. Tears rolled down his cheek as he struggled for control.

"Truly," the General's voice added.

"What are we doing about this, sir? He's going to take us all out."

"Calm down. He's one man."

"Sylvia makes three. Wylie's no normal man, either. He's a perfect killing machine. Please. Please, help."

"I'll see what I can do."

"Thank you, sir."

Mathew didn't feel better after he disconnected, but it did feel good to be doing something. Maybe he could help in some way.

A gust of wind rattled the glass in the window near him. It startled the doctor so much that he jumped and gave a partial yell.

"This is ridiculous," he scolded himself. "I'll just live at the office. With their security, I should be safe."

Dr. Turner, headed to his room to pack.

PRESENT DAY: Detectives Jewels and Joe

Near the end of the day, Joe grabbed his jacket and stopped by Jewel's desk. He interrupted her typing.

"Hey, Cara wants me to ask you to come over."

"Tonight?" Jewels looked at him.

"Why not?"

"Because I have all this to do." She indicated her keyboard.

"Balance, Jewels. Remember? This can wait. You've got all the important points already. We'll see you at 6:30."

Jewels forcefully exhaled air. "Do I need to bring anything?"

"Just yourself," Joe said with a smile. Then he turned and walked away.

She stared at his retreating back and said, "Damn."

She didn't see Joe's smile widen as he pushed through the exit.

PRESENT DAY: Detectives Jewels and Joe

At 6:30 sharp, Jewels knocked at Joe's front door. She dressed casually in jeans and a nice long-sleeved sweater. It was a lavender shade with white swirls delicately patterned throughout. The color complimented her dark tresses.

A young, beautiful blonde opened the entry. She too wore jeans and a sweater; her top was of a white and champagne pattern. Her hair hung in silky waves past her shoulders, and her make-up was applied perfectly.

"Kaylee. You're home." Jewels beamed at her.

The teen laughed. "I haven't seen you for a while, Jewels. I thought it would be nice."

"It is very nice, Kaylee. "

"Well, come on in. Mom and Dad are in the kitchen."

Jewels smelled the garlic, onions, and cheese cooking and followed the scent. When she entered the kitchen, she saw Joe buttering French bread and adding garlic salt. Cara was peeking into the oven.

"Hello, Jewels," Cara said with a smile. "Prompt as usual."

Jewels grinned. "Hi, Cara. Thanks so much for the invite."

Joe said, "Do you want cheese on your garlic bread? I'm going to toast these." Holding a tray of French bread.

"Yes, please."

"I hope lasagna is okay," Cara said.

Jewels looked at the five-foot four-inch woman and smiled. The attractive brunette smiled with her green eyes twinkling. She was curvy but slender. Her dark hair spiraled down to her mid-back, a perfect example of what a woman should be. She was an exact complement for Joe's large frame.

"Oh, I love lasagna. Especially with garlic cheese bread. It's been forever since I've had any, too."

"Same," Kaylee said. "I love it, and Mom doesn't make it that often." She sat on a bar stool, close to the activity but not in the way.

"Hey, Kaylee, why don't you set the table, Hon?" Cara asked.

She reluctantly complied.

"What can I do?" Jewels asked. She fidgeted slightly.

"Just sit there and look pretty," Cara said.

Joe scoffed, and Cara smacked him. Jewels just laughed.

Joe said, "You do need to relax. Everything else is taken care of."

"How can I relax with everyone working but me? Let me get the drinks, at least."

"Just try relaxing a bit for once," Joe repeated.

"Kaylee is getting the drinks." Cara said. She popped the bread into the oven. "Aren't you, Kaylee?"

"Sure, Mom." She looked at Jewels and grinned. "What do you want, Jewels? Lemonade? Tea? We've got several cans of soda, too."

"Water is fine, thanks."

Kaylee set a glass in front of Jewels, water with lemon.

Jos said, "We had a feeling that you'd want water, so Cara bought some lemon for you."

Jewels smiled with a slight widening of her eyes and said, "Thank you.It smells divine."

"Just wait until you taste it," Joe said with a wink to his wife.

"Oh, my God, Mom. This is the best one yet!" Kaylee said. She closed her eyes in ecstasy as she chewed. "Ummmm."

"It's just because I haven't made it for a while, Dear," Cara said, but she smiled.

"Outstanding," Jewels said after swallowing her bite. The flavors were still dancing on her tongue.

"I still say you need to patent and sell this, Sweetheart. Wow." Joe said.

Cara giggled. "Oh, stop it," she said. "But thank you, everyone."

Kaylee brought out a game. "Do you like games, Jewels?" Kaylee said, hopefully.

"Dad said you need help with having fun."

Jewel's eyes slid over to Joe. He held his hands up defensively.

PRESENT DAY: Wylie

The military dubbed him "The Chameleon" while on a mission. They gave him a shield that allowed him to

146

blend in with the scenery. In stealth mode, it was difficult to tell that a man was present.

Wylie is what he went by if his handlers were trying to humanize him. He smiled, but the expression didn't reach his eyes. It was all a farce. They considered him no more human than their vehicles.

The press called him "Eat Your Heart Out Killer." He rather enjoyed that one. Only those who earned his wrath were played with so vigorously, but the nickname amused him.

A lot of research went into Wylie's construction. He was the ultimate machine. Near invisibility, implanted access to information and languages, infrared and thermal detectors, x-ray vision, and could run up to forty miles per hour for sustained periods. Wylie also appreciated the protective magnetic fields in his palms that repelled fired rounds and opened locked doors.

When he looked back to the man he used to be, in truth, Wylie couldn't deny that he *did* feel gratitude to his creators. His current body was much more powerful, a lethal weapon. Nothing could stop him from killing when he willed it. And with Yellow Charge, he was invincible.

The problem was one of control. His creator gave him a brain filled with implants and cutting-edge technology. They hadn't planned on his self-awareness and independent thought.

Because of the cure-all pill, Yellow Charge, Wylie had a better grasp of who he was now.

He was Wright, with a lust for revenge, and now transferred to him. Though, his anger was beginning to diminish. Now, the annihilation of those who experimented on him felt more like a mission.

Whether his heart was in the next target or not, he was determined to be Wright tonight. He would become the man he once was. Afterwards, he'd process his feelings and decide where to go from there.

Wylie had no doubt that he would finish the mission. The Army got that part right. The soldier's brain that was now his was programmed to never give up. Whether he finished in clone body number one or twenty-seven, the mission would be completed. Even if Wylie orchestrated the operation himself, once it was fed into his awareness, it became a compulsion that couldn't be denied.

He was learning a lot about being a real human from watching the detectives. He had to give them credit. They were connecting dots faster than anticipated.

His pulse increased slightly as he admired Detective Polten's mind... well, her in her entirety. She was damned attractive. It pissed him off that his brain wasn't programmed for sexual activity. Maybe with time, the Yellow Charge would heal that, too.

The man with many names turned his thoughts back to his mission. He noted a car trailing the target.

They had a tail on the doctor, Not that it would do him any good. Once he targeted a person, they were as good as dead.

The Chameleon pulled over and let the blue Avalon pass. He activated his binocular vision and watched as the car pulled into a driveway a few blocks down. A white car, parked conspicuously in front, announced the residence was under police protection.

They didn't realize that the more challenging a mission was, the more likely he was to engage. The thrill of the kill was motivation, but the true exhilaration came from stalking the quarry.

The Chameleon smiled. The traveling duffel lay to his side, full of needed weaponry. He'd keep surveillance as he waited for night to fall.

A few hours later, a dark blanket covered the world, and a few soft stars twinkled merrily. Wylie prepared. Just before exiting his vehicle, he slid a yellow capsule into his mouth.

"Base this is car 72, Hamilton speaking. Nothing to report at this time." He sat quietly in the surveillance car, constantly scanning for activity.

"Keep an eye out, Hamilton. He's good. You won't see a thing until he hits. Do frequent walk-arounds with weapons drawn until your relief gets there," his superior advised, "maintain hourly contact."

"Yes, sir."

"Hamilton?"

"Yes, sir?"

"Do you have your infrared technology with you as you were instructed?"

"Yes, sir."

"Monitor it. Constantly."

"Yes, sir. Hamilton out."

The cop on the night watch was a man in his early-thirties. Sitting outside of a residential home wasn't the most rewarding of jobs, but it was a necessary duty if he wanted to work his way up the ladder. With military combat training, he felt overqualified.

It was a simple surveillance job. His lieutenant acted as if this were a combat mission, but he was merely monitoring a doctor's house for possible threats.

Yes, the rogue soldier had a high skill level, but it must not be that dangerous if his superiors sent him solo.

Hamilton retrieved a Snickers from his brown paper bag. He didn't notice the heat signature quickly approaching. Before he took a bite, a hunting knife was at his throat.

"How... did you get here without being seen?" he managed to croak.

"I'm The Chameleon. Didn't they tell you?" Wylie hissed in a soft, raspy voice. Hamilton could feel his menacing laughter as Wylie slit the young man's throat.

The assassin's smile broadened when he noted his heat signature did not register with Chameleon mode activated.

"This is going to be fun."

Michael Teigha, fresh out of the shower, flipped on his television. He enjoyed a few programs before drifting to sleep. It helped keep his mind off his job. He was so driven to stay at the top of his field that he rarely allowed his brain a break.

He glanced at the picture on his nightstand. A dark-haired beauty smiled at him, a little girl with chestnut curls on her lap. Michael's heart flipped a few times as he stared at them. He missed them dreadfully. He planned to finish this project in the next six months then join them in their beach house on the East coast.

The bed creaked as he adjusted and punched his pillow into the appropriate shape. He turned his attention to the program. Mere minutes later his eyelids began to droop.

A gloved hand gave him the remote. Michael almost thanked the person before fear squeezed his heart, as he tried to scoot away.

"Hello, Michael." A shadow man appeared out of thin air. "If you yell, you will not be heard. Do you understand?"

Michael gave a quick nod.

"We can do this fast and easy, or slow and sweet. The choice is yours, but you will not survive the night," said the shadow.

"Wh-what do you want?" Michael stammered. He sank back into the pillows as far as he could.

"I want the chip technology," The Chameleon said.

"And then?" Michael croaked.

"And then I'll eat your heart," laughed the shadow.

PRESENT DAY: Detectives Jewels and Joe

"We've got another hit," he announced as soon as Jewels breezed into the office,"Let's go."

"Let me guess. It's a doctor," Jewels said, still winded.

"How did you know? Are you psychic or something?"

"Who is it this time?" Her expression was deadpan.

"Michael Teigha. He worked on tracking devices."

"For the military, right?" The corners of her mouth turned down.

Joe pointed at her with his index and his thumb up, in a shooting gesture, and applied a smirk to his lips. He said, "You nailed it."

"Do we need to question the military?" She teased, her eyes glittered dangerously.

Joe replied with a shrug, "If we only had the power."

Jewels pursed her lips and pointed a finger at him. They left the precinct and got into their car.

"Good thing I haven't eaten yet," Jewels said.

"Yes, but coffee can come up just as easily," Joe said.

From a block away police lights ignited the scene. Police tape had cut off a large area, and road barricades were in place.

"What's with the unmarked?" Jewels asked as they pulled up.

"There was a detail on Dr. Teigha last night. The officer is also deceased."

"This guy *is* good." Jewels craned her neck to see the car better.

"To say the least. There's no telling what we have on our hands if the military's involved. I'd say we have a super soldier," Joe said quietly.

"That's a scary thought." Jewels nodded.

"Agreed."

They walked toward the unmarked vehicle. Officer Lars stood by on protective detail.

"Has the policeman also had...?" Jewels couldn't ask the entire question.

"No, only the poor doctor. It's not pretty, but the cop escaped with only a sliced throat," Lars stated.

The detectives viewed the man in the front seat. Jewels swallowed to prepare herself for the even more gruesome scene ahead.

The forensics photographer was just leaving when they entered. He looked a little green.

Joe was close by, and Jewels took comfort in that fact. She followed him as he veered toward an officer with a clipboard.

"Anything missing that you can tell, Burns?" Joe asked.

The officer looked over his notes. "Yes, we've got a laptop missing and probably more. The victim was home alone, but his office was thoroughly ransacked. Someone was obviously looking for something."

"Thanks," Joe shot a meaningful look at Jewels. He said in a lowered voice, "We may be in over our heads."

"Agreed," she said, swallowing hard. The site was worse than Jewels imagined.

It wasn't a typical murder scene in any sense. The doctor was killed in his bedroom, but there was blood splatter in every room, even closets.

"The sick-o dragged the victim's body into every room to play with it," Joe said, "and ate pieces of his heart along the way."

Jewels covered her mouth to keep her coffee down. Deep breathing would not help with the stench of blood.

Joe said, "I think we've seen enough. I want a list of missing items when you return," he said to Officer Burns who gave a curt nod.

Jewels meekly followed Joe, struggling to hold in the contents in her stomach.

"Uh, Joe?" Jewels called.

"What is it, Jewels?" His eyes grew wide as he read her expression.

"Look." She pointed.

A bright yellow lemon, completely free from blood, sat on a bookshelf close to the front door.

"Th - that wasn't there when we walked in."

Joe scratched his head. "I didn't notice it there, either, but Jewels, it had to be. Who would break into a crime scene just to put a lemon by the door?"

Jewels didn't answer but shuffled forward again. Once out of the house, they removed their plastic protection and tossed the pieces into the crime scene trash. Jewels took a few long, deep breaths in the car.

"I'm sorry. It's just–," she began.

"You don't need to explain," Joe said. "This is the first exposure we've had to this level of deviancy. No apology is necessary."

"Joe. But it's not just the blood. I can't get that lemon out of my head."

"You think our killer had something to do with it?"

"I have to wonder. Maybe that's who dropped lemons off by my house."

They rode in silence back to the precinct.

PRESENT DAY: Dr. Bellamy James speaks to General Hawkins

The General's phone rang. His office was filled with high-ranking officers.

"General Hawkin's office. Colonel Landers speaking."

"I need to speak with General Hawkins, immediately," said Dr. James.

"Who's calling?" the officer asked calmly.

The doctor snapped, "Tell him it's Alfa 12 Gamma Ray, and this is urgent!"

A moment later, the general's gruff voice came on.

With no pleasantries, Bellamy said, "General, The Chameleon's gone rogue. We need assistance."

"You doctors can't control your own experiments?"

"Hey, our experiments are under *your* direction, sir," Dr. James said. "We do what you pay us to do. It's the military in charge here."

"What do you require?" said the general after a long sigh.

"Help. The Chameleon is targeting all the doctors who are involved with this program. I could be next!"

The general's line was quiet a few moments. "I'll send some guys to protect you. We will find and neutralize the experiment. This time, follow protocol. Put in the damn kill switch."

"Yes, sir." Dr. James replied quickly, "Thank you, sir."

"There's no way you can activate the frequency to make him explode while he's still living, is there?" Hawkins asked.

"No, sir. If there were a way, he'd be gone."

"This project is incredibly important. This is the key to victory and eventually an end to warfare."

"It's important to me, too, sir. But my life is at stake."

"Noted. I'll get some men out there in two hours. When we get Wylie back, see about making a kill switch using the same tech in the Electro Rounds. We don't want to leave cloned bodies as evidence if we kill them."

Bellamy said, "Yes, I'll get on that."

The general added, "I think if super soldiers realize we can permanently remove them at any time, those who considered going rogue will rethink."

"Yes, sir." Dr. James added, "Oh, and sir? There's one more thing you should know."

"What is it?"

Dr. James said, "He killed Dr. Teigha. He now has access to Teigha's home data."

"Teigha had tracking information, what about soul frequency data?"

"Sir," Dr. James said, "he had it all."

"Damn it!"

"If Teigha has a back-up file somewhere, we're okay. We'll need to find a new technician who is good at duplicating what we've got."

"On it."

PRESENT DAY: Wylie

Currently, Wylie secured a room in a basement. The elderly couple didn't keep up with current events. All they cared about was the rent they charged was paid in cash.

Wylie propped his head on his hands and stared at the ceiling as he lay on the small mattress and processed his last kill.

Dr. Teigha offered no challenge: didn't fight back at all, and handed over the data without delay, and he'd even offered up a secret bunker if he agreed to kill him quickly. Wylie was all too happy to comply.

Wylie considered Teigha's body and his treatment of it. And it bothered him. Was he actually... feeling remorse? Teigha seemed mild mannered; a man just doing his job. He obviously cared for his wife and child.

Wylie promised himself that he'd become Wright for this kill. He'd wanted to see if any of his old emotions would surface. Once the man was dead, Wylie felt strangely dissatisfied, even disgusted with himself.

158

There was a pattern emerging. The Yellow Charge truly was a miracle drug. First, it allowed him to recall his former life. Then, he remembered his vow of revenge and how much that emotion consumed him. He'd felt the grips of the compulsion. Now, though, after many more capsules, he felt the old personality receding. *So, what was he left with? Who was he now?*

One thing for certain, Wylie knew he was still a mission-driven soldier. The compulsion to follow orders didn't diminish, so Wylie knew he'd see his goals through to fruition. The confusing thing was... he'd evolved into something more than a mere machine, *but to what degree?*

He was finally human: a man. A man with emerging feelings... and needs. Wylie wasn't sure if he liked it or knew how to handle it.

The soldier's mind turned to the detective. *Jewels.*He wondered how she'd liked the gift he left for her.

For tonight, Wylie wasn't focused on eliminating doctors or destroying military personnel. Instead of murder, he allowed his mind to be drawn elsewhere. Thoughts of a pretty police detective filled his head as he drifted to sleep.

PRESENT DAY: Detectives Jewels and Joe

Jewels had enough for the day and shut down her computer.

"Jewels?" Joe said when he noticed her slipping on her jacket.

"Yes, I promise. I'll keep my Glock by my side at all times."

"If that lemon was a present from our man, I would prefer it if you stayed at our house. Let me call Cara. I'm sure it won't be a problem."

"No, Joe. It was just a lemon."

"Jewels. It wasn't just a damn piece of fruit. It was a *message*. You know it. I know it, and more to the point, he knows it. Just what that message is worries me. Is he still toying with us? Is he showing he can dance around without us even knowing? Or Jewels, is he becoming fascinated with you? That's particularly scary."

"Joe, if he were trying to hurt us, he could have done so long ago. I'm sorry I overreacted. I'm sure it's nothing." Jewels slung her purse over her shoulder and jangled her keys in her hand. "Good night. I'll see you in the morning."

"Text me when you get home. Call if you need anything," Joe said. "And I mean, any time of the night." .

"I promise. Good night."

PRESENT DAY: Wylie

Wylie found a functioning old Jeep at a salvage yard and swapped the tags with a random vehicle. It was perfect for blending in on a military base. He waited until 3:00 a.m. and returned to base.

He parked the Jeep away from his target area. The Chameleon moved like the wind, and a short time later, he stood at the entrance and studied the fortified doors.

Most heavy locks were magnetic. And Wylie had magnetic shields in his hands and frequency codes in his brain. The security on a level 4 clearance facility was no match. Wylie held his hand to the locks and the door opened with a soft click. He walked right into the secret laboratory where it all started and headed directly for the cloning lab.

For a moment, Wylie could do nothing more than stare. It was disorienting to stand among bodies who were all exactly alike.

Exactly like... me.

Wylie's internal scanner gave him information about each. He found the controller for the clones and duplicated it into his mental files.

He pointed the remote to the most developed clone. He unhooked the monitors and helped his twin to his feet. They silently made their way to the Jeep and then to his safe house.

Teigha had made a deal. If Wylie agreed to kill him quickly, the tech expert would not only hand over all the technology data, but he'd also disclose an unused place, safe from discovery.

The refuge was at the back of property Teigha purchased discreetly. The specialist was a paranoid bastard, for sure. He made a bomb proof shelter with thick walls, security measures, and enough supplies to last for months.

Along one wall, were piles of food rations including emergency dried meals in plastic containers, huge vats of water, and storage units full of a variety of protective gear. There were cots and blankets resting against the back wall along with propane and kerosene tanks. Assorted camping gear including a gas cook stove and lanterns were arranged neatly in one corner.

Wylie admired Teigha's plan to keep his little family safe should Armageddon arrive. He could remain here, comfortably, for an awfully long time.

Wylie guided the mindless clone to one corner and sat him in a folding chair. He prepared cots for the two of them.

A FEW DAYS LATER: Wylie

For the first time in his short life as Wylie, he'd become truly fascinated with someone besides his targets.

Detective Polten. *Jewels.*

She was beautiful, smart, and determined. The combination intrigued him. In either life, he'd never really been interested in women. Now that he had found one, he could do nothing about it.

When he was Wright, he'd not been interested in physical attention. He hadn't as Wylie, either, until recently. He wondered vaguely if it had something to do with his new, more physically fit body or with the healing powers of the Yellow Charge.

The problem was two-fold. He was a wanted man in many ways, so he'd never get to enjoy a relationship as a civilian. Oh, he was sure the detective wanted him, but not in the way he was beginning to imagine. Then, as a mission-minded soldier, his body wasn't ready to follow a non-operational, personal directive such as… sex.

So, he satisfied his fascination by watching her.

He didn't want to harm her, but he didn't seem to be able to stay away. He watched as she pulled into her drive and parked. The slight but curvy woman got out of her car and entered her home. He followed her inside.

It was about 11:30 a.m., and she went straight to her fridge and pulled out a small package of salmon. She prepared it with some rice and a small salad. She grabbed a beer and prepared a place at the table. When she sat to eat, he moved closer, towards her handbag.

He pulled a small plastic bag from his pocket and slipped it inside the purse.

Wylie froze when the plastic crinkled. He watched as the detective stopped eating and cocked her head. She pivoted in her chair to look toward the bar. Wylie didn't move a muscle. He realized he was even holding his breath.

Slowly, Jewels rose from her chair. She unholstered her gun and held it in front of her. She turned her head both ways to check her peripheral then focused on the bar as she took cautious steps forward.

Wylie slowly withdrew his hand from her purse. The bag moved minutely with his action, and the alert official immediately grasped her gun with both hands in a tight grip.

"Who's there?" she asked.

Wylie held his hand in front and activated his shield in case she decided to fire. He had to be careful because hadn't taken a Yellow Charge.

She came around the bar in a crouched position with the weapon in front. When she didn't see anyone, she straightened, lowered her arms slowly, and let out a pent-up breath.

"I'm going crazy," she whispered. She placed her gun on the counter and her eyes were drawn to her handbag. She saw the tip of a plastic bag.

"What the?"

She pulled the bag out slowly and gasped.

Jewels looked around again before walking to the table. She grabbed her phone.

"Yeah, Joe? Can you come to my house? Um, I've got something to show you. Make it quick, please."

<><><><><>

When Joe arrived, Jewels led him to the table. Her unfinished meal was pushed to the side while a baggie containing something odd sat in the cleared space.

"What the hell?" Joe asked.

"It's some kind of … microchip." Jewels said, holding the bag up before him.

The bag contained a tiny metal chip with pieces of dried flesh sticking to it.

"Holy hell." Joe wiped a hand across his forehead. "Where did you get this?"

Jewels looked up sheepishly. "That's the funny thing, Joe. It's really creeping me out. It was in my purse."

"What?" Joe's eyes widened. "What do you mean, it was in your purse?"

"Okay, so I got home to make some lunch. I sat down to eat, and I could have sworn I heard plastic crinkle. I turned and saw my purse move slightly. It was the weirdest thing. I drew my gun. That's when I found the baggie."

"Did you clear your house?"

"Um, no. Just the kitchen."

They worked as a team and swept the home. When they returned to the kitchen, Joe sat down in front of the chip.

"Where else have you been today?" Joe asked, examining the technology through the plastic again. "I mean, where could someone have slipped that into your purse?"

"That's the thing, Joe. You know I've been at the precinct all morning. It had to have been there, unlikely, in my car, unlikely, or here, also unlikely. You tell me. Unless the guy's invisible and is standing here listening to us, I can't imagine when or where."

"You didn't stop and run into a grocery store?"

"Nope. I drove straight here."

Joe was silent for a few minutes before he finally said, "You know what I think this means."

Jewels shook her head. "Joe, I infringe on you all enough."

"Your safety is paramount."

"No, Joe."

"I insist. You stay with us until we can find out more about this killer. I don't want you staying by yourself after this." He rattled the bag for effect.

"Do you think we should contact someone?" Jewels asked.

"Besides the chief, I wouldn't know who," Joe replied.

"Want me to give the Army a call?" Jewels laughed.

"Very funny," Joe said. "Though, I imagine they would want their technology back. Whatever this thing is."

The detectives left, the air shimmered and a man appeared. Wylie sat in Jewels' chair and reflected on his recent actions.

It felt good giving Jewels the secret technology. For the first time in his life, Wylie felt a warmth surge through him. A few moments later, he smiled and stood. He activated his shield as he shut the door to the detective's house behind him.

Later that day, Jewels headed toward Joe's desk.

"Have you decided what we should do with that chip, Joe?" she asked. "It keeps nagging me."

"No. I'm not quite sure *what* to do with it. Part of me thinks the military will find out we have it when we start testing it, but I'm sure I just have an overactive imagination."

"I don't know. This whole thing is surreal. I think we should just sit on it a few days."

Joe looked at her. "Until we know what to do with it, that seems wise." He paused a few minutes before asking, "What time will you be over tonight? Do you want me to go to your house with you to pack?"

"Joe, really. This isn't necessary."

"Oh, yes, it is," he said. "You're family, Jewels. We all insist: Cara, Kaylee and I."

"Joe, I never want to be an imposition. I would feel in the way."

"Better in the way than dead, Hon. Eat Your Heart Out is making a point by slipping that into your handbag. Then there's that lemon... and the bag of them. This guy may be pointing us in the right direction, but at the same time, he's saying, 'See what I can do? You can't catch me.' It's downright disturbing. To tell you the truth, I'm spooked. Obviously, more than you are."

With a leveled gaze she said. "Joe, you're making a mountain out of a molehill. It's not that big of a deal."

"Are you kidding me? Did you hear what I just said?"

"Alright, alright. I'll come over, dammit."

Joe was too worked up to smile. He wiped a hand over his forehead and said, "Thank God."

"Dad, Jewels is here," Kaylee said excitedly.

"Sweetheart, we know you love Jewels," Cara said, "but give her some space. They have a hard case they're working on."

"Can't we play more games while she's here?" Kaylee asked with a pout.

"Maybe sometimes, but not tonight," Joe said. "Honey, we're pretty stressed."

"But games can be stress relief," Kaylee said. She peered out the window. "Oh, and she's bringing pizza."

"She didn't have to do that," Cara said.

Why don't you go out and help her bring in her things?" Joe suggested.

Cara said, "I'm sure she'd appreciate it."

Kaylee needed no encouragement to dash out the door to help Jewels. She returned carrying three pizza boxes.

Joe took the boxes. Kaylee had a duffel over her shoulder.

"You feeding an Army?" Joe asked. Then he chuckled. "I guess I could have found a better metaphor, considering."

Jewels grinned back. "Yes, yes, you could have."

"Is this all you have?" Cara asked, taking the duffel from her daughter.

"For now."

"What do you mean, for now?" Joe asked. "If you're planning on going back to your home, do not go alone."

"Joe…"

"Jewels," Cara joined in, "Your safety comes first."

"Yeah, Jewels," Kaylee said. "We care about you too much." Kaylee waited a moment before bursting, "I'm so glad you're going to stay!"

Jewels opened the pizza boxes. "I thank you all very much for your concern. It means a lot to me. Now, let's eat before it gets cold."

PRESENT DAY: Wylie

Wylie wasn't sure how to feel. He clenched his fists a few times. Air whistled through his nostrils as he watched Jewels disappear into Joe's house. This... unreasonable anger he felt at her decision to stay with her partner really bothered him.

Was this what people called jealousy? No, Wylie scuffed. *Most were in a relationship for that emotion to arise, right? Then, why do I want to kill Joe with my bare hands? He's done nothing. I think my feelings against him are what bother me most. He's not part of the mission, so why this desire to destroy him?*

Wylie revved the Jeep and headed out of town. Once he arrived on the property, he hid the vehicle in a copse of trees, switched on Chameleon, and headed for Teigha's secret hide-a-way.

Wylie stood his clone in the corner of the bunker as he prepared for activation. He accessed the replicated device technology and programmed his soul's frequency into it. Then he retrieved two yellow capsules of the healing formula.

"I'm not sure how this is going to work out, Bro," Wylie said to his clone. "I'm going to activate you with my own soul's code. I have no idea if my soul will stay within this body, leave mine for yours, or break in two pieces. If it's the latter, I hope we both make it through."

His mirrored image said nothing, merely stared into space. Wylie chuckled and patted the man's chest a few times before he slipped a Yellow Charge capsule into his mouth. He swallowed one himself.

"I got you, Bro. We're in this together. Get ready. I hope this works!"

Wylie pushed the internal button. A high-pitched frequency resonated throughout the room. Wylie tried to hang on to consciousness, but in the end, the edges of his vision frayed, blackened, and both men were swallowed by darkness.

A psychedelic tunnel appeared on the horizon of Wylie's awareness. It grew exponentially. It seemed nearly alive as it swallowed him whole. Moments later, Wylie found himself in a chamber filled with white light.

He saw a tiny sliver of light trailing through the tunnel. It was attached to him, yet he couldn't touch or remove it.

Wylie heard a sound echo through the living tunnel, a siren's song, beckoning for his return.

Wylie sat, though nothing solid held his weight. He was simply... there.

When he stood there was a dense white fog at his feet. The air shimmered with hints of color.

Soon, another siren's song began, joining with the first. The duet's melody was in perfect harmony and so beautiful it made Wylie's eyes water.

Wylie continued forward and noticed a break in the field of white mist. When he drew closer, he saw a shiny pool of thick liquid. A green and yellow shimmer covered the surface and misted the air above the pool. He reached to touch it.

The substance attached to Wylie's finger and replicated the shape, blossoming backward. Once a hand was constructed, forearms began to take shape. Soon, a new body emerged from the liquid and stood before Wylie.

It dried and hardened. The shimmery green and yellow mist floated above the figure. It began to transform into something more substantial. As the mist tightened, an iridescent ball emerged that radiated the green and yellow more intensely. It slowly lowered itself onto the top of the figure's head. With a crack, a hole opened in the shell, and the shimmery substance slid inside.

After a moment, the hardened material began to glow first green, then yellow. The light began to pulsate, like a beating heart. Finally, the hardened crust burst with a poof.

The new being stepped forward. It quickly resumed the coloring and posturing of a human: a mirror image of Wylie himself. The clone dusted his hands and looked up. His eyes met Wylie's.

"Hello," the new being said.

Before Wylie could respond, the tunnel reappeared and sucked them up, like a giant vacuum hose, and thrust them back into their physical bodies.

When he came to, Wylie noticed he and his identical twin were lying on the floor. Wylie crawled to his clone and felt for a pulse. He breathed an audible sigh of relief when he felt a steady beat. Gently, Wylie shook his twin.

Slowly, the man's eyes opened. "Whoa," he rasped. "No way!"

"Oh, my god! I'm two men at the same time," Wylie said. Although he'd suspected this might be a possibility, he never really expected it to happen.

His shadow nodded agreement. The clones stared at one another. They were one mind in two bodies. Wylie could talk to the clone, like talking to himself. He knew what he was thinking before he could say it. In fact, speech wasn't necessary between the two.

"This is really weird but freakin' neat!" the new man said in Wylie's voice.

"So we don't get confused, what do you think about the name Wayne?" Wylie asked his mirrored image.

"It's good, but you knew that." They laughed.

The two men settled into lawn chairs. For a bit of time, they just looked at one another in awe. It was so strange to have a connection with someone on such a deep level. It never happened before. Ever.

Now? Wylie thought, *I have a real brother. We're truly of one flesh and soul, and our connection is genuine. And I'm feeling something... Is this happiness? Is this what it's like when people have family?*

"The Yellow Charge - ," Wylie began.

"Is curing us on all levels," Wayne finished with a nod.

Wylie said, "I had no idea such a formula could heal our minds. With every capsule, I... *we* change."

Wayne laughed. "Our bloodlust is nearly gone, now."

"Isn't it strange - that we can kill on a mission..."

"Because it's our job," Wayne said.

"But the desire to mutilate is gone," Wylie said. "That was who Wright was. Now we've broken that bond, finally. I no longer desire to eat hearts."

What a revelation. I have no desire to kill for revenge or to cannibalize. I am totally free.

"I think that last dose of Charge did it," said Wayne. "It was a double dose."

"Because the bond we share doubled the healing power."

They fell silent for a few moments, pondering their new revelation.

"I wonder," said Wayne, "what would happen if only one of us took the charge..."

"Would it protect and heal both of us?" Wylie finished.

"But it's best not to tempt fate," laughed Wayne. "And you know, we are nearly free. We're not there quite yet."

"Yes, Bro. First, we've got a mission to complete."

"Okay, so you already know my plan," chuckled Wylie.

"Yep," said his soul brother.

PRESENT DAY: Dr. James

"Sir, there's been a break-in at the lab," Sam said as he met Dr. James in the parking lot.

Police sirens screamed as military police sped to their location.

"Was anything taken?" Dr. James yelled over the noise.

"You'll have to determine that."

"Why?"

Sam looked at his feet sheepishly. "Because they broke into the cloning lab."

"Oh, shit!" Dr. James was dumbfounded.

"No damage," the technician stated. "Though security was breached."

"How in the hell did that happen?"

"We can't figure that out. It's like he said the magic words, and the doors opened wide."

"The gifts he has... shouldn't have worked on our own facility. Shut these alarms off so I can think!" Dr. James snapped. "And secure the doors back to the lab."

"We've already done that, sir," Sam said. "We know how important your work is."

"We also have to intercept the police. They are not cleared for this level. Take Pattinson and head them off. Just... make up something about the damn alarms."

"On it." Sam grabbed Pattinson, and they ran toward the commotion.

Dr. James muttered, "I need to get the general back on the phone."

<><><><><>

Dr. Bellamy James's voice was loud, "General, we have an emergency."

"Another one?" came the gruff voice. "What is it this time?" He sounded bored.

"The Chameleon stole a clone!"

"What? You're sure?"

"Sir, respectfully," Bellamy replied, "I know exactly how many clones I have."

"How many are ready to deploy?" asked the general sharply.

"I have five soldiers awaiting souls, sir. I had six."

"Prepare them for activation." General Hawkins commanded.

Dr. James replied, "Sir? They're physically ready, but we don't have the souls. Scheduled executions of their inmates are months away."

"Not anymore."

"Sir?"

General Hawkins snapped, "Prepare your units for activation ASAP. And this time, place their damn trackers better. Shove them up their asses if you have to. Whatever it takes so they can't be removed."

"Of course."

"And James? Put in kill switches using Electro formula. Leave no trace. Understood?"

Bellamy inhaled sharply, "Understood."

The general continued, "By activating these soldiers, we'll kill two birds. They'll track down Wylie and protect you... and this experiment. I hoped to take The Chameleon alive, but right now I would settle for vaporized."

Dr. James said, "I want him alive too, General. But your point is well taken."

"This is our ticket to fame, doctor. Are you sure you're the one capable of maintaining control of these... um, men?" the general's tone softened. "You understand Mathew is no longer able to run the operation from within. After the loss of his daughter... You're in -charge when I am not there."

"Yes, sir," Dr. James replied carefully. "I can step up. The problem with Wylie is that his soul was once a career killer. He has gone back to his roots. These new inmates are evil, no doubt. They'll be killing machines, for sure, but they're much more controllable than Wylie. We didn't know at the time of his activation the soul's original personality would come through. We've made corrections since in the five that are ready to go. These soldiers will be mindless. We've just installed chips in their brain to mildly shock the personality section if it becomes active. I'll just need to add your suggestion... the Electro formula tied to the termination frequency... the um, kill switch."

"Good. Make sure you do. We can't have another incident."

"Yes, sir."

PRESENT DAY: Detectives Jewels and Joe

Jewels lay wide awake in the guest bedroom. It was decorated gender-neutral for whomever might stay there. The walls were a heavy cream color complimented by deep champagne curtains. A few interesting pictures hung on the walls. The floor was an original warm oak partially covered with a decorative rug to keep toes from complaining on cold nights.

Jewels had no criticism with her friend's hospitality except they didn't take no for an answer. The problem was she wasn't in her own bed. That fact alone made her unable to sleep. In addition, she'd unknowingly been near a murderer. Not just any murderer, either. Eat Your Heart Out. That too made it impossible to quiet her mind.

She tried deep breathing. Just when she was finally on a cusp of sleep, an interesting thought jolted her wide awake. It was as if someone injected her with stimulants. She picked up her phone and did a little research. Her heart beat harder and heavier in her chest; it was just as she suspected.

Although it was nearly one in the morning, she texted Joe.

Joe. You up?

She threw off her covers and paced the room. Nervous energy raced through her body like Indy cars.

No response.

Jewels slipped into her robe and house shoes and went to the kitchen. She needed a drink for her suddenly dry throat. She filled a glass and sat at the table.

A shuffling noise sounded from behind her. She turned to see a very tired Joe entering the room.

"Can't sleep?" he asked groggily as he slid into a kitchen chair.

"Hell, no."

Joe peered at her from underneath his sleep-swollen lids. "You already have coffee or something?"

"No. Joe. I've made a connection." Her fingers were woven together and her thumbs twirled.

He sat across from her and rested his elbows on the counter. He leaned forward eagerly.

"Sylvia Turner is the daughter of a doctor."

Joe scratched his head. "So, it explains her career interest in the science field?"

"Joe. This means she wasn't the primary target. She was the *daughter* of the primary target."

"Who's her father?" he asked. His voice slowly returned to normal.

"Dr. Mathew Turner. He's a death row psychologist."

Joe sat taller in his chair. "So, you think Eat Your Heart Out was one of his patients?"

"I'd bet money on it. Do you remember that horrid phone call?"

"Of course."

"She screamed, but then they had a conversation. We couldn't clean up the audio to know what was said, but only after they spoke did he kill her. I can't figure out the military connection, but we need to have a talk with Turner senior."

"I'll contact the evidence team and see if anything interesting turned up at his daughter's house," Joe said.

"Let's also revisit the place. Maybe we can dig a little deeper. Our killer likely targeted her because she knew something about her father. Maybe he's looking for something her father gave her."

"I'll get a team to help search. I'll make sure they know we're looking for hidden evidence. They may not have searched the attic or under the house. I mean, they probably just thought it was a murder scene."

Jewels tried to calm her breathing. "We are onto something, Joe. I know it."

"I agree. But let's get someone else to crawl under the house. I'm too old."

Jewels laughed. It broke the tension on her face. She said, "I'd almost pay money to see that."

"You better not."

"You know," said Jewels thoughtfully, "Sylvia's connection on the murder fits his M.O. now. I mean, he usually only targets experts in the field, but he hit her for a similar reason. She was not random like we originally thought."

"Yes, and I'll bet her father is on his target list."

"Agreed."

"Now," said Joe. "Drink some chamomile tea or something. I'm going back to bed."

She smiled. "See you in the morning."

<><><><><>

The next morning, Jewels woke excited, despite her restless sleep.

"Good morning." Cara said as Jewels walked into the kitchen. "Coffee is ready. Breakfast is cooking."

"Wow, Cara. You don't have to wait on me. I'll wear out my welcome faster if you're my servant."

"Nonsense. I enjoy cooking for those I care about. You won't hear Joe complain about it."

"Speaking of Joe…"

"You're speaking of me?" He said as he shuffled into the kitchen.

Jewels smiled. "Wow. Déjà vu."

"Yeah, that's what I was thinking," Joe said with a big yawn.

Cara raised a brow.

"Jewels had a revelation last night about the case."

"Oh, how wonderful!" she said. She flipped an omelet. "I hope it breaks it wide open."

"We hope so, too," Jewels said.

Cara placed a huge omelet on each of their plates.

"Ummm, this is as delicious as I knew it would be," Jewels said as she took a second steaming bite. "Thanks, Cara."

"Truly, my pleasure."

Yellow police tape was still protecting the crime scene. Three men and a woman on the search team helped the detectives scrutinize the entire premises thoroughly. Jewels and Joe searched the main level along with Officer Rodriguez. Officers Lars and Burns worked the crawl spaces, and Officer Walsh the attic.

In the bedroom, Jewels rummaged through clothing and personal effects. Joe searched kitchen cabinets, and Rodriguez investigated the bathroom.

"Nothing in the bedroom," Jewels said, walking into the kitchen.

"I haven't found anything of interest, either." Joe said.

"How's it going, Rodriguez?" Jewels asked.

"Oh, there're lots of interesting things in here," he said, "but nothing pertinent to the case."

"Guys," came a muffled female voice. "up here."

They hurried up the ladder in the hallway. Officer Rodriguez climbed to the top and was handed a fire-proof safe.

"I bet this has something in it," Joe said.

"It's a good possibility," Jewels said. "I mean, it's hidden and locked. Something's in there."

"Let's get it back to the station right away."

At the station, Joe made short work of the lock. He handed Jewels the files inside, and she took them to her desk to analyze.

"What did you find?" he asked a bit later.

"Just a bunch of notes," Jewels said, "I don't understand them, though. A lot of scientific terminology, a bit over my head, but something's definitely here. A girl died over these. I think we need to find someone discreet to help us decode them."

"First," said Joe, gently taking the papers from her, "We make copies."

"Hey, Joe, before you go..."

"Yes?"

"Turner mentions a Dr. James and a general. That could be significant."

"General...?"

"His name is General Hawkins," Jewels.

"We may have just found our military connection," Joe said.

<><><><><>

Jewels sat at her desk with a cup of thick, oily coffee. She scrunched her nose at each swallow.

"Hey, Joe," she called.

"Yeah?"

"I want to visit Turner today, but what do you think about visiting James first? He's sort of on our way."

"Sounds good. Our killer strikes at night. If we make it a priority before this evening, I don't think the order matters much."

She nodded and took another sip. Her nose crinkled again.

"Why do you make yourself drink that stuff?"

"I don't know. Why do you?" She grinned.

"Because it's there."

"That's as good of a reason as any."

"Well, put some sugar in it at least, then."

"I did."

"Well then, put *more* in it."

Jewels's grin widened.

"So, where does this elusive Dr. James work?" asked Joe.

"The base. That's all I can figure out. One day a week, he volunteers a few hours at the military hospital."

"Does that day of the week happen to be today?"

Jewels grinned again. "Why, yes, it does."

"Leave within the hour?"

"No problem."

The Detectives entered the military hospital.

Joe approached the receptionist. She had dyed auburn hair and kind eyes. She looked at him expectantly.

"We need to speak to Dr. James, as soon as possible," said Joe. He showed his badge.

"Dr. James is very busy right now. Are you certain this is urgent?" she asked.

"Very certain," Jewels said firmly.

Five minutes later, a frazzled man with bright orange hair made an appearance.

"Come with me," he said and led them to a small office with a desk that took up over half the space. "Please, sit," he said, indicating two metal chairs.

The doctor remained standing behind the desk.

Dr. James began. "How may I assist you?"

"You've heard of the killer targeting doctors, I assume?" asked Joe, getting straight to the point.

"Um, yes." His eyes were large behind his military-issued glasses. He leaned forward and placed his hands on the desk.

"Well, we're slowly connecting the dots," Joe continued. He allowed some time for this information to sink in.

"And you tie into this somehow," Jewels added.

Dr. James straightened and asked, "Why do you think I'm in cahoots with a killer?" His tone was astonished, and his surprise appeared genuine.

"It's not that we think you're working with him," began Joe.

"It's that you may know more about him than you're letting on," continued Jewels. "In other words, we believe your life may be in danger." Again, the detectives allowed the power of their words to sink into the silent room.

Finally, Dr. James blurted, "Well, I have nothing to do with any of this!"

"Are you sure about that?" asked Jewels. Her finely arched brow rose even higher.

"Pray tell what you're talking about," Dr. James exclaimed.

"Does this look familiar?" asked Jewels.

She held up the microchip in a clear evidence bag. The chip looked rusty and had a few hairs attached.

Dr. James's eyes widened. "Wh - where did you get that?" he asked. His voice cracked a little, and finally, he sat behind his desk.

Rather than answer, Joe asked, "What is it?"

"I - I, um, can't be sure," the doctor replied evasively. He lurched back to his feet and reluctantly accepted the bag Jewels handed him.

"What do you *think* it could be?" Jewels pressed.

The doctor held the baggie up so he could better view the chip.

When no answer was forthcoming, Jewels continued, "Let me tell you what *I* think. I think this is a microchip that came out of some soldier who is now plotting revenge on a group of doctors for some reason."

"And we believe you're a target," Joe said.

"Uh, wh-where did you... find this?" Dr. James repeated.

Jewels and Joe shot a glance at each other.

Joe said, "Your soldier friend delivered it to us."

"Holy shit," the doctor said. He dropped the chip onto the desk with a small clatter, and at the same time, he dropped heavily back onto his chair. Immediately, Doctor James leaned away from the offending technology.

"At first, we thought he was toying with us," said Jewels. "You know, the bad guy telling the police, in not so many words, 'Ha ha, you can't catch me'? Well, we believe, instead, that he *wants* us to know more."

"Know more?" echoed the doctor mechanically. His eyes seemed to glaze over.

"Yes. We know the military is involved, and we believe this is a rogue soldier on the hunt for those who may have experimented on him." Joe studied the pale man before him. "We don't think he wants us to stop him, but he wants the experimentation stopped."

"Experimentation?"

"Our guess is that you were exposing him to illnesses and then used cryogenics to heal him," Jewels suggested.

Dr. James's eyes widened. His skin drained even more color.

"And we think you must have found a cure for him, and now he's pissed that he was ill in the first place," Jewels added, "so now he's seeking revenge."

Jewels went with her gut based on how the doctor was reacting to their theories. Police often stated their hypotheses as though they were facts, but sometimes, improv got answers.

Shakily, Dr. James stood. "I - I don't know quite what to say. To say the least, you've thoroughly shocked me. It sounds like a silly conspiracy theory a teenager would believe. It certainly doesn't sound like something that would come out of the mouths of two detectives. Now, if you will excuse me."

"We're not finished," Joe said.

Dr. James insisted, "I don't have time to listen to this. We're quite busy."

"Preparing to ward off an attack from a murderer?" asked Jewels. One eyebrow raised slightly in accusation. "Listen, I don't know how you're involved, exactly, but you and Dr. Turner are on this guy's radar. We found some notes when we went back to Sylvia Turner's house. She didn't know she had them, but somehow, her father had slipped them into a safe and had it hidden in her attic. In fact, we believe that's why the 'Eat Your Heart Out Killer' targeted Miss Turner. We believe he was after that data."

Dr. James rubbed his chin. His eyes kept flitting to the phone. Finally, he said, "We need those notes."

"They are under police protection as evidence," Joe informed the doctor.

"We're saving lives here," Jewels reminded, "That's what's important."

"I guess I can ask the chief if we can make copies for you, though," offered Joe.

"Fine."

Joe nodded. He stole a glance at Jewels. They'd achieved a level of confirmation: the doctor knew a lot more than he was revealing.

"So, will you tell us about this device?" Jewels asked again, picking the baggie up from the desk.

"I'm sorry, I can't help you with that," Dr. James said.

"Okay." Jewels sighed deliberately. "Maybe you can't." She dropped the bag into her purse.

"Our next stop is Dr. Turner. Maybe his memory is better," said Joe with a slight snort.

When the police took their leave, Dr. James began frantically punching numbers on his phone.

"So… who do you want to go see now?" Joe asked. "Do you want to proceed to Turner's or drop back by Dr. Montrose's?"

Jewels said, "We need to see Dr. Turner. After what we discovered about him, who he may have records on, and what happened to his daughter, that puts him a priority."

"Spot on. We're both on the same page, then," said Joe.

"I hope he'll cooperate. If we press him, maybe he'll recall who he's counseled that could be holding a grudge."

"Yep," said Joe. "I'll bet there aren't too many inmates running around loose that he's counseled."

"He'll know exactly who's after him," Jewels agreed.

Joe continued, "I know that Dr. Montrose wasn't shooting straight with us, but I also feel the government or rather, the Army, is holding him back. They were clearly experimenting on people with cryogenics. They must have used some magic pill the military has dibs on. Dr. Taylor suspects the same, about the cure all pill. My guess is that we won't get any new information out of him. Let's go ahead and put Montrose on the back burner."

Jewels gave a nod.

"So, do we have to get clearance to visit the prison?" asked Joe.

"Luckily, no. I guess he has an office downtown as well. Hopefully, we'll find him there."

A short time later, the detectives parked and walked in the facility. Dr. Turner was clearly expecting them. He quickly ushered them into a room that reminded the detectives of a counselor's office. There was a plush sofa and matching chair, a table-lamp combination, and decorative pillows strewn around. There was even a beanbag or two on the floor.

"Doctor of psychology, I presume?" asked Jewels with a smile.

"Yes, I'm Doctor Turner," he answered. He nervously returned Jewel's smile and shook both detectives' hands. "I'm a licensed psychologist, but I don't practice in this office."

The detectives looked at one another in surprise.

"Are you working full-time right now?" Jewels inquired.

Dr. Turner said, "Um, yes. I work at the prison counseling death row inmates."

"Then, why do you have this office?" Joe asked.

"I don't plan to counsel the unsavable population forever," he said. "I keep this office in case I have someone in a functioning society who needs a session; also, because it's ready for me once I decide to resign at the prison. It's a premium location, and I don't want to lose it. Plus, it has good security."

"Ah," said Jewels. "I'm glad we caught you here."

"So, why are you here, now?" asked Joe.

"Well, as you probably know… my, um, daughter…" Dr. Turner's voice faltered then trailed off. The psychologist stopped to scrub his face. They respectfully gave him a few moments.

"Yes, sir. I'm sorry for your loss," Jewels said sympathetically.

"Sir, we wouldn't be here if we weren't trying to stop this killer from striking again. We believe you could be a target," Joe said apologetically.

"Yes, most definitely," Dr. Turner said. His voice trembled again. This time from fear. "Honestly, I'm staying here day and night. I haven't been to the prison for a week. I'm afraid to go home, afraid to leave."

"Can you help us?" Jewels asked softly. She leaned toward him to stress her sincerity. Her dark hair swung forward like a silk curtain with her plea. "We need more insight into this guy. We've got to know the facts in order to stop him."

The scared man quietly said, "My hands are tied with some information. It's top-secret military stuff, but I'll tell you what I can. If you want to schedule a time to come back, I can have the military representative here."

"I understand," soothed Joe. "Do you know why you're being targeted?" His hazel eyes met the doctor's darker ones directly.

"I believe it's because I'm part of a government science project," Dr. Turner responded. "To divulge much information, again, I'd have to have a military security officer present during a police interview."

Joe nodded. "Until we can arrange that, maybe you can help with what you *can* share. Our goal is to stop this guy from striking again, and any information to help point us in the right direction can only help."

The psychologist nodded.

"Why is this killer trying to stop the program?" Jewels asked, relieved the doctor was receptive to a mild interview.

"I don't know why he went rogue," Dr. Turner said. "You'd think he'd be a little more... grateful."

"He's a soldier, I assume?" Joe asked.

"In a way," Dr. Turner admitted. "Look, I can't say more about him than that... but if you want to come back, I can get those here that need to be. I didn't know you were coming, or maybe I could have had someone here already. But... he does have a lot of training with weaponry. I suppose you already knew that though."

"Hum," said Jewels.

"We understand," Joe said.

"But this soldier… he wasn't experimented on, was he?" pressed Jewel. Her rapt attention was focused on the doctor.

"Like, you didn't inject him with diseases and try different types of remedies on him," Joe's face was carefully neutral, but distaste crinkled his eyes as he asked the question.

Dr. Turner's mouth opened a bit in surprise. He stared at them as they threw questions in his direction.

"As in treatments using cryogenics?" Jewels added.

"Certainly not!" declared Dr. Turner indignantly. "We may run the border on some things we do, but that's unethical. I save lives."

"What do you do for the prison?" Jewels asked. She deliberately leaned back to give him space.

Dr. Turner's face reflected mild relief. "I told you, I counsel those in need. There are some mandatory programs those in the general population have to attend, but I'm also there for the death row inmates."

"To counsel?" Jewels pressed. She leaned forward slightly to indicate her interest.

"That, and just to listen," Dr. Turner confirmed. "Sometimes the most you can do for those who aren't ready to change is just to be there for them and plant seeds."

Jewels nodded in agreement.

"When you're there, you also study their behavior." Joe said and carefully watched the doctor.

"Um, well, yes," the doctor admitted. "That's part of a counselor's job. Once you get to know your clients, you can see when they're upset and can try to intervene." He shifted uncomfortably in his chair. "It would be difficult not to in that setting."

"That's true," Jewels said. "We, too, study behavior." She paused for a moment to give him a pointed stare. "However, was studying his behavior part of an experiment?"

"I can say that I did evaluate behavior and reactions of the inmates for research purposes. You can look up my work. I publish articles on my findings."

"So, that leads me to my next question. Were you also counseling this soldier, the killer?" Jewels asked.

The man in front of them didn't seem surprised by the question. "In a round-about way, I guess you could say that," Dr. Turner said.

"What does that mean?" Joe asked. He adjusted his tall frame as he addressed the man.

"How do you counsel in a round-about way?" Jewels asked. "I would think that was a straightforward question... yes or no."

"I'll get right to the point. Did you target him for an experiment based on his behavior?" Joe asked.

Dr. Turner cleared his throat and said, "I wish I could explain further, but that's classified."

"Can you tell us if this guy is pissed at you?" Joe asked.

Dr. Turner lifted his brows as he considered the question. He answered, "He has no reason to be."

"Did you have anything to do with this?" Jewels asked, holding up the chip in the evidence bag.

Dr. Turner's reaction was more fabricated than that of Dr. James. He acted surprised, but his response didn't reach his eyes.

"I record frequencies onto chips," he said at last.

"What kind of frequencies?" Jewels asked.

"I can't say." The doctor's face whitened even more, and he began to fidget in his chair.

"Classified?" Joe guessed.

"Yes. Look, does the Army know you have that?" Dr. Turner asked.

Joe straightened to his full height and said, "I haven't made a point to tell them."

The doctor gave a tiny nod.

"Do you know why the killer would send us this?" Joe asked, indicating the chip with a shake of the bag.

Mathew took in a breath before replying. "Really, I don't. He should know that civilian detectives don't have power over the military. It doesn't make sense." He shook his head with confusion.

"That's kind of what we thought," Joe agreed.

"So, it made us consider possibilities," Jewels said. "We think he's just trying to let the authorities outside of the military know that something unethical is going on. I can't think of any other purpose."

Both detectives studied the doctor.

"That's *very* interesting," Dr. Turner finally said, "and... strange." Those last words he mumbled to himself.

"Why do you find that strange, doctor," Joe asked, "if he believes what is going on is immoral?"

"Um," Dr. Turner began, once again clearing his throat nervously, "because doctors give second chances at life. I would think that anyone who had that second chance would be grateful instead of resentful."

The partners stood.

"Agreed. Well, thank you for your time. Here's our card," Joe said, stretching his arm forward to place it on the edge of the desk, "in case you think of more you *can* tell us."

The psychologist breathed out a small sigh of relief. He reached for the card and slid it into his desk drawer.

"Thank you," Dr. Turner responded. He shook their hands again.

Joe said, "We'll see ourselves out."

PRESENT DAY: Dr. Bellamy James

"General, we may have another problem," Dr. James said into the phone. "Wylie sent a couple of detectives his microchip."

"What?" bellowed General Hawkins.

Dr. James held the phone away from his ear.

The military man continued to rage, "What in Christ's name is wrong with that boy? I thought you and Turner checked him out well before using him in our project!"

"Sir, like I said, we didn't know the personality of our subjects would also be reincarnated," Dr. James explained again. "We thought we were just powering a lifeless body with the internal fire to ignite the clone's functioning. We had no clue the former personality would also hitch a ride. Now we know, and the next group won't have this issue."

"Are you ready to activate them?" the general asked impatiently. "I'll buzz you at the time of the inmate's termination so you can invoke the frequencies. We must activate them as soon as possible. These will be the men to take out The Chameleon. They'll be stealthy... and have no ties to us as they don't exist."

"Yes, sir. They're ready. What will you do about the detectives, sir?"

"You leave that to me."

Dr. James just received a new production of ten cases of Yellow Charge from The EPDP and Dr. Montrose. He lovingly called it the "Superman pill". Even if a person were knocking on death's door, it could heal every ailment from broken bones to stage four cancer in a matter of moments. It also gave the user superhuman strength and abilities. A person could, literally, jump off a building and walk away healed.

Bellamy was irritated that Wylie got off with eight cases of the drug. He shuddered to think what Wylie planned to do with so many pills. Surely one rogue soldier couldn't last that long. *Maybe the Chameleon would succeed with the pill's aid.*

Dr. James gave each of the new clones a dose of Yellow Charge. The general arranged the termination of all the targeted death row inmates for precisely the same time. Dr. James didn't ask questions because he didn't care for the answer. It was no matter: the men, in essence, weren't really dying. As far as he was concerned, they were being brought back to life in a new body.

His phone buzzed, indicating that the time had come. Dr. James and his assistant activated the five new frequencies. The soldiers were strapped up this time to avoid what happened when he stimulated Wylie.

Precisely ten minutes later, he and his assistant began reviving the clones. It took a bit of time to unstrap all the men and get them acclimated to their new bodies, but soon all five were standing at attention. Dr. James found himself the focus of five emotionless sets of eyes. A chill shivered down his spine.

Bellamy drew in a breath and counted to ten. Then, in a voice of authority, he addressed the clones. "Men,

General Hawkins is your superior. He has an assignment for you."

"Why is the general not here to present the job in person?" asked the first activated man, One. The clone's dark eyes narrowed as he assessed the orange-haired man standing before him.

"He's engaged with another section of this assignment," Dr. James answered, straightening his six-foot frame. "He's given me the power to be your liaison. I created you, and I command when he's unable."

"What's the task?" asked Three.

"To take out this target." The doctor held up a picture of Wylie.

The soldiers gathered around to see the representation of the man.

"Sir, he looks like us," Four responded.

Dr. James smiled. "Yes, men, he is one of your clone brothers gone rogue."

"Rogue, sir?" asked One.

"He is not complying with orders," Dr. James explained. "We've rectified his issues with you men, but we need to correct the problem with him. In other words, he needs to be, um, rewired. He's gone off on his own mission and is targeting his creators."

The five surrounding the doctor straightened and tensed their muscles. Their nostrils flared.

The second clone, Two, said, "Sir, going against an assigned mission isn't permissible."

"That's just what I want to hear, and that's why you're here, soldier," Dr. James said. He turned and fiddled with the remotes. "You'll have to look with your technology rather than your eyes since Wylie's identical to you all in nearly every way. I've internally assigned you his frequency. You should sense it... about... now."

The men nodded as one.

Number Four said, "We've received the frequency, sir."

"If I may, in what ways is the target different from us?" asked Number Three.

"It may help us locate him quicker," added Five.

"The biggest thing that is the difference, soldiers, is your brain functioning. His wires got mixed up and he's off mission. You have, um, protections in your head to prevent the same from happening. In addition, you all should be aware, you each have a kill switch."

No one spoke for a few moments. Finally, the men nodded as one.

Two asked, "A kill switch?"

"That simply means that should one of you go off mission, then we don't have to have a lot of men hunting you, like we are Wylie. You will be terminated and reincarnated into a new clone body."

Then men stilled. Dr. James looked from one to the other.

Finally, Two cleared his throat. "Sir? We have Wylie's frequency, but it's dead."

"We've done so well with anti-detection devices, even without Chameleon Mode. He, ah, won't appear on your radar until the target is within three-hundred yards of you. So, you'll have to go to places we believe he's marked in order to find him." Dr. James's glasses mirrored identical silhouettes in the light as he looked around at the men. The reflection hid his green eyes from the soldiers' perusal.

"We only have a range of three-hundred yards?" echoed One.

"You can see much further than that with your super vision, soldier, but his specific frequency won't track unless you're close to him. The evasive technology we've installed in each of you works very well. You must be within range for the technology to filter through the other protective encoders."

Dr. James took off his spectacles and wiped the lenses. "Three of you will be with me, and the other two of you will be assigned to Dr. Turner."

"Protective detail?" One asked.

"Your job is to seek and detain. But, yes, you're on protective detail for Dr. Turner and myself. Wylie is after us, and we need to survive. Your job is to protect us and bring in Wylie."

"Alive or dead?" asked Four.

Bellamy looked at the man and said, "If possible, alive. If not possible, take him down."

"Yes, sir," the five soldiers said in unison.

"Our lives are the priority; apprehending Wylie is the second. Even if you nearly kill him, that works. We can use Yellow Charge to revive him," Dr. James ordered. "Make sure you're in confidential frequency. No civilian should be aware."

"Activate Chameleon Mode?" asked Three.

"Yes," the doctor confirmed. "Do you know what that is?"

"Sir," said One. "We are programmed with projection abilities that we can activate at will."

"Those projections are really prisms of ultraviolet rays that alter the way light refracts and is absorbed," continued Two.

"Very good," said Dr. James. "Do you understand how that can help you?"

Five said, "Yes, sir. The light prisms alter the wavelengths of visible color and distort it so that we can blend in with the background."

"Becoming invisible, if you will," added Four.

"And to what degree would you be invisible?" Dr. James asked. "You know Wylie will know what to look for."

Three said, "To a civilian, we are completely invisible. To military personnel equipped with an understanding and knowledge of the shield, we would only be detectable if they caught our movement which would look like a slight ripple in space."

"We appreciate this invaluable tool," Two said. "It's an assassin's dream."

"Highly effective," agreed Three.

"You are welcome," Dr. James said. "Of course, those with your frequency locks can 'see' you at all times."

"Even if we're further than three-hundred yards away from your machine, sir?" asked One.

"Yes. Remember, you're not trying to elude one another. He's removed his chip, and yours is permanent, so you don't need to stay within that perimeter. It's a vital part of your body's operating systems."

The clone brothers' eyes locked on one another.

PRESENT DAY: Dr. Mathew Turner

Mathew slid a thick packet of classified papers into a large yellow envelope. Before folding and sealing it, he added in a few tiny microchips of several varieties. A few were the type he implanted in the base of the inmates' brains to measure activity, and a few were tracking devices. Still others were the special technologies that offered visual readouts, Chameleon mode, supervision, translators, and magnetic manipulation. He taped the envelope shut then, braving his fear, got in his car.

PRESENT DAY: Denten Smith

Denten spent the afternoon tidying his small apartment near the downtown strip then people watched before making a simple dinner. He was surprised when his doorbell rang.

The young man peered through the peephole, unlocked the door, and swung it open wide.

"Dr. Turner. What are you doing here?" His eyes were wide, and he let out a pent-up breath.

"Please, shut the door." Dr. Turner said. He jumped when he heard the elevator ding from down the hall.

Denten closed the door. "Please, come in and sit." He led the way to his living area and sat in a recliner. Dr. Turner sat on the mismatched loveseat on the other side of a well-used coffee table.

"So, what brings you to my house, Doctor? I'm surprised to see you."

Mathew licked his lips and looked out the window for a few minutes.

"Can, uh, I get you anything... to drink?" he asked.

"Denten, I - I need to tell you something." Serious brown eyes swung back to look at him.

"Yes?"

"I don't really know how to say this. You're not in danger, or anything... but I am."

"What do you mean?"

"You know what our work has entailed. I really don't know if I should be discussing this here... I hope to God they aren't bugging your place."

"What? You're not making any sense. And, frankly, you're kind of scaring me."

"Denten, remember our first soul transfer?"

"Of course, I remember. That day was magic. That's the day we made history."

"That day I sealed my fate. I signed my death warrant."

Denten straightened and went still. "Please, Dr. Turner. What are you talking about?"

"Wright Miller. He's in the body of - "

"Wylie. I know."

"He's in the body of Wylie, but... Denten, he remembers."

"He... remembers?"

"Uh, yeah. He remembers his former life. *Wright's* life. And he's out to get me."

"Oh, my God." Denten stood and began pacing. Suddenly, he stopped beside his windows and pulled the shades. "Are you telling me... you have a super soldier after you? A military weaponized assassin?"

Dr. Turner cleared his throat and shifted in his chair. "I - I believe so."

"And you came... here?"

"Denten, he isn't after you. He murders for revenge, and Wright didn't know you."

"Dr. Turner, he's killed those who are associated with the experiment. You know that."

"Okay, okay. I, um, wanted to save what I could. I truly don't think you're in danger, but I am, and so is my life work. I, ah, want you to have it."

Mathew offered the thick envelope to Denten. His young assistant tentatively put out his hand .

"That's all of it. It's my research, my documentation of the subjects, and the microchips we've installed in them. Really, all you're missing is the clone body and Yellow Charge. If, um, something happens to me, you can continue my work, if you want. But the general will be a source of contention. You'll either have to work with him again or start over somewhere far, far away."

Denten leaned back. His eyes were wide, and he simply stared at his supervisor for some minutes.

"You're trusting me... with all this? But why?"

"Yes. I'd have given it to my daughter... but... well, you know why I'm not. You're the closest thing I have to a family. And... you're like the son I never had. If I happen to survive, and we apprehend Wylie, I'd like that back."

"But... you don't think you will."

Dr. Turner's head dropped until he was looking at the floor. His elbows were propped on his knees.

"Sir? I'm honored you chose me. I promise, I will make good on all this. You trust me, and you chose *me*! You can count on me to see this through, but... I want us to do it together."

"So do I, Denten, so do I."

"Dr. Turner, I'm a little freaked out right now. Do you, ah, think you were followed?"

"We'd know it if I was," Mathew said, standing. "Well, thank you, Denten. I'll be going now."

As the doctor was opening the door, Denten called to him.

"Sir? Thank you. And, be careful."

PRESENT DAY: Detectives Jewels and Joe

Joe pulled into the drive. He looked over at Jewels and said, "Pretty productive day."

She shrugged. "Yes and no."

"We have more information than we did," Joe pointed out.

"True, but we didn't make a huge headway. I wish I knew what to do to protect those men, but I'm torn. In a way, I can sympathize with Killer for wanting to prevent them from doing experiments on others."

"Yeah, but killing is never the answer."

The corners of Jewels's lips turned down. "No, you're right, and I didn't mean to imply otherwise. I feel for them in one aspect, yet in the other, they deserve the fear. However, Dr. Turner's pain over his daughter... no one deserves that."

Joe nodded. His forehead rumpled, and Jewels was sure he was thinking of his own teenager. They got out and went inside.

Cara and Kaylee were in the kitchen frying up small pieces of battered chicken.

"What's going on?" Joe asked. He came up behind his wife and hugged her. Then, he tweaked his daughter's nose.

"We're making Cashew Chicken, Dad," Kaylee said excitedly. "It was my idea. Jewels likes Cashew Chicken; she told me so."

"Well, I like it, too," Joe said with a laugh. "Thank you, ladies."

"That's very sweet, both of you," Jewels said. "So, what can I do to help?"

"If you and Joe want to set the table and pour drinks, that would be great. Then just sit and visit while we finish up," Cara said with a warm smile. "Your workday was longer than mine."

About thirty minutes later, the group enjoyed a warm meal with the best of company.

"Any progress on your case?" Cara asked. She took a sip of her milk.

Joe said, "We've made some headway."

"But things will hit a turning point soon," Jewels said. "and that worries me."

"Are you guys safe?" Kaylee asked. Her hazel eyes were wide. They shifted back and forth between her parents and her idol.

The detective's eyes widened when she realized her mistake. "He's not targeting us, so yes, we're safe."

Kaylee's shoulders raised slowly. "But... you're staying here."

"Yes, Honey," Joe said. "She's staying here at our insistence. I just don't want to take any chances. From what we've learned, though, this guy has specific targets. We aren't on his list."

"But Dad. How do you *know*?" Kaylee's hazel eyes were shiny, and her pink lips trembled slightly.

"In a way, he's told us so," Jewels said. "He had to have been close to me to give me some messages. He never touched me or acted like he might."

Cara leaned back and was studying her husband and Jewels. She didn't say anything, but thoughts were racing behind her green eyes.

"What?" Kaylee asked. Her eyes were large when she pressed her hands into the table. "Did you see this guy? Why didn't you arrest him?"

"We can't talk about anything more," Joe said. "But honey, I promise you, we're safe."

Jewels got up and began clearing the table. She picked up the plates and carried them over to the counter by the sink. It was a welcomed distraction from the seriousness of the conversation. Cara got up and joined her.

"But..." Kaylee said.

"Sweetie, wipe the table down for me," Cara directed.

"Oh, okay, Mom." Kaylee's shoulders drooped. Then she brightened and said, "At least I don't have to do the dishes."

"No, you don't," Jewels said. She plugged up the sink and began running hot water. "You made supper. Cara, you and Kaylee go sit. Joe and I've got this."

Joe cocked a brow then grinned. "Nicely done," he said. He pushed back from the table and walked over to the sink.

"You can pre-rinse them and give them to me. Then, I'll wash and hand back to you to rinse again."

"Sounds like a plan," Joe said with a wink.

While they were at the sink with the water running, Jewels whispered, "Sorry about that."

Joe nodded. "No worries."

Cara put up the drink containers while their daughter wiped the table. Then they sat and watched the other two work.

"This is so nice the way you all work together," Jewels commented as she handed Joe a plate to rinse.

"It certainly is," Joe agreed. "It makes life worth living, having a family to share it with." He looked meaningfully at Jewels.

She laughed and then asked, "So when are we going bowling with the department?"

"In two weeks. I set it up for a Friday night."

"Okay. Sounds good."

Joe looked at Cara. "It's a family night, too, so I'd like you two to plan on coming. I think most of the precinct will bring his or her family if they can."

"I'll go if Jewels can bowl with me," Kaylee said.

"I'll definitely bowl a game or two against you."

"We'll be on teams, so Jewels will be on our team the entire night, but you'll still have to share her, Hon," Joe said.

Kaylee stuck out her bottom lip, but her eyes were smiling. "Oh, alright."

PRESENT DAY: Dr. Mathew Turner

Dr. Turner shut the lights in his office. He was glad he'd purchased such a comfortable couch since he'd be sleeping on it while Wylie was on the loose. He thought again about how the man had been given a second chance at life.

He truly didn't understand why Wylie wasn't grateful. Yes, the man had been incredibly adamant when professing he didn't want to be experimented on, but Mathew just couldn't understand why anyone wouldn't be grateful for a second chance...

Or thankful for what I've managed to accomplish, he thought.

They'd given Wylie *life*. Wright had been *reborn*! How many people got a chance to start over with a clean slate, especially when he was on death row?

I mean, thought Mathew, *how many dream of immortality? Damn, the man should have been more grateful!* the doctor shook his head.

The turning point for the reborn man, Wylie, had been when they insisted that he have the tracker replaced. To Mathew's knowledge, that request marked the beginning of the clone's rebellion.

Bellamy pondered the soul's entrance into a new body. At birth, all former life experiences were wiped away. A child had to begin with a new slate although past lives' karmas still had to be repaid. Never in his wildest dreams did Bellamy think that when an old soul transferred into a new body that the personality and its life knowledge would accompany it.

So, what did that mean for karma? Did Wright's karma follow him when he became Wylie? Mathew had no clue. The merging of an old soul with a new brain presented a whole new realm of possibilities that he hadn't thought possible. The only way to find out was to document, but how was he going to do that?

Wright's personality had become increasingly apparent within the cloned soldier. It was subtle at first, but now it'd made a full-blown appearance. *At least the new clones shouldn't have that problem with the chip inserted into the brain.* If their minds ever tried to usurp control, the personality sensor of the chip would destroy the attempts with mild shocks.

In theory, the stolen soul's only job should have been to power the clone and make him self-sufficient… to a degree. They weren't supposed to remember their past lives. The general wanted the soldiers mindless, merely a blank slate consumed with whatever order it was fed. The only thinking the soldiers were supposed to do was survive and react to war situations. Otherwise, they were to eat, sleep, and function as needed to stay in prime shape; pondering life was not an option.

Dr. Turner shook his head. *Was it that life simply wasn't enough? Maybe the soul needed a purpose? In children, boredom can breed destruction. They also need structure and guidance. Was this also true with a reborn man?* It was a lot to consider.

Mathew grabbed a drink from the glass next to him and lay back on the couch. He tossed and turned a bit. It was going to be one of those nights where sleep was evasive.

"Hello, Dr. Turner," said a low voice right beside him.

The doctor jumped and tried to sit up. An unseen hand held him down. He felt the fingers digging into his chest and collar bone.

"Stay where you are," the voice commanded.

"Wylie?" Dr. Turner whispered.

"Yes."

"Why, Wylie? We gave you life!" he blurted. "Why are you killing all who helped you?"

Wylie turned off Chameleon mode. A normal-looking man in uniform appeared before Dr. Turner. He was exactly six feet and extremely fit. He radiated power. His brown hair was shaped by a crew cut and his dark eyes processed all details in a glance.

"Respectfully, sir." Wylie began. "You *didn't* help me. You were helping yourself while trying to control me. No animal likes a cage. So, I'm taking the liberty to free myself."

"You'll never be free, Wylie," Dr. Turner said. "The Army is too big to fight. If you surrender now, we can resolve this."

The clone shook his head and smiled. "I have a plan, Good Doctor." He winked. "I need you to tell me where you keep all your data."

Mathew swallowed and shuddered. "You know I can't give it to you, Wylie."

"Oh, I think you'll find that you can. You see, the human body can only take so much pain," Wylie said with a smirk. "Once a certain threshold is reached, you'll willingly do anything I command. Unfortunately for you, the military educated me with optimum types of torture to extract information in a very short time."

The doctor swallowed audibly. "Wh - why do you want the data?"

"I want the data because I'm going to make my *own* version of a cloned Army," Wylie said with a chuckle. "Then, I'll destroy the data to make sure the experiment isn't repeated."

"Why, though, Wylie?" Dr. Turner asked. "Why does it matter so much to you?"

"Because no one should dictate someone else's life. You're resurrecting us to die, again, for you. And my guess is to die again and again, for you. That's hell, Doc. Even manufactured men deserve respect and to be valued as human." He let his words sink in before adding, "And I don't think you'll want to relive *your* death."

The meaning wasn't lost on the doctor. "I - I if I give you this data, w - will you…"

"Take it easier on you?" Wylie said, grinning now. "I think that can be arranged. But that's only if I get *all* the data, and copies."

Mathew sat up and scrubbed a hand through his hair. Slowly, he stood to his feet and shuffled to retrieve the data. He was silently escorted.

"Wylie?" Matt said softly. He clutched the files tightly to his chest.

"Yes?"

"I'm telling you this as a courtesy. So, um, please use the same courtesy with me…" Mathew cleared his throat. "They've activated five new clones, and they're looking for you."

The soldier smiled. "Yes, that earned you brownie points, Doc. I'll tell you this as a courtesy to help relieve your mind. I am no longer Wright. I have no desire to eat your heart."

"Wh - what?"

"Those Yellow Charge pills truly are remarkable," Wylie said.

"They've... they've healed you from your revenge?"

"Yes, Doc, it appears so. Your experiment with the soldier's brain was successful, though. I will finish what I started."

With shaky hands, Dr. Turner handed over the files. "What will you do with a cloned army? Where will you get the souls?"

The experiment said, "The purpose of the army is to help destroy experiments like this one conducted by the military. I'll have all the souls I'll need."

"How?" Although Mathew's voice shook, his curiosity was strong enough to question the assassin.

The soldier shrugged and said, "My own soul is a reflection of who I am."

"A - Are you... saying... you're going to use your own soul on *multiple* clones? You don't know what you're doing!" gasped Dr. Turner. "You don't know what'll happen if you rip your soul!"

"Why, yes, I do, Dr. Turner. I'm not really ripping my soul into pieces," Wylie said with a lengthy laugh. "Of course, I didn't know what would happen before I tried it, but really, what I did was *replicate* my soul; it was not damaged."

"How?" Mathew gasped.

"I'm Wylie, but I'm not," he said with a laugh. "I called my second self 'Wayne'. I stole a clone from the lab."

"I don't believe it! Y - You're… Wayne?"

Wayne took out his long, military blade. "Believe it," he said. "And nice to meet you."

<><><><><>

As Wayne finished in Dr. Turner's office, he sensed a threat.

"They're here," he thought to Wylie. *"I sense two."*

"Kill both and head back here with the data," Wylie responded. *"If you can, feed their frequency to me right before you terminate. We can imbed their souls in the embryos I've started."*

"That's the plan." He was sure his brother knew he was grinning.

Dr. Turner's facility was a large, multi-story office. On the first two floors were counseling agencies. The levels above that were for equipment, resources, data, and research labs.

Wayne turned on Chameleon mode though he knew it was no protection against other clones. He popped a Yellow Charge, prepped his M16A4, and began to hunt.

At this hour only the clones would be here. He had just crept around a corner when rifle fire splintered the doorway in front of him. Wood and drywall exploded, and powdered smoke filled the room. Splinters pelted Wayne's skin.

He fell back and took cover. He would have to let them come to him; it was too risky otherwise. Although he had taken a Yellow Charge, he was sure his adversaries had, too, so with two to one odds, there was a good possibility that he'd be apprehended if he weren't careful.

"You'll have to pick them off by hand, one-by-one," Wylie said in his mind.

"I got this, Bro." Wayne took position and scanned for threats.

He saw a flash in the corner of his eye. The first clone burst into the room and rolled behind some cabinets. Wayne returned the rifle fire with his M16A4. Then, the window from behind shattered as opponent number two made his entrance. Wayne turned his rifle to engage the new threat. Gunfire ricocheted from everywhere as the identical men fought each other.

One clone was hit, so Wayne seized the opportunity to roll from his spot and finish him. Already, the man had healed, but Wayne was too close to prevent his escape. He delivered a lethal stab.

"It's a good thing you have these self-sharpening blades from the bunker," Wayne thought to his replica. *"Adding the sealed Electro formula to the knife tip is the only way I could have killed this guy."*

"Yes, Bro. I think it's the only way to annihilate anyone amped up on Yellow Charge. Bullets take too much time to reach our hearts, but the blade tip slammed

in the heart with the electro formula is just too much for even the Yellow Charge to heal."

Wayne mentally transmitted the downed-soldier's frequency to his soul brother. When he turned around, the second clone was there, his rifle centered on his heart.

"Lower your weapon, Wylie," the identical man said. His voice was flat and emotionless though a bit breathless. "I must return you to the lab."

Wayne laughed although his fists were clenched. "Do you really think so?" he asked.

The man replied, "Yes, I do. I'd rather it be alive, though."

"Look, man," Wayne began. "You can be free of this leash that binds you to the military. Do you want to be human again? I'm sure you don't want to be a mechanical slave to them forever. Think of what your life will be like."

"Soldier, I have no choice."

"You have to make it your choice. Otherwise, your life will be boring and mundane. Yes, there is excitement in killing, but is that all you want out of life?"

Wayne lunges to the side, aiming to position behind a metal wall unit. At his sudden movement, the opposing soldier opened fire. The bullets ripped up the floor underneath him as they tore into his flesh. His body knit a web around the burning bullets as they entered his body. The healing force of the cure-all pill allowed the process to look like the bullets were hitting him and then falling to the floor. The warrior felt energized during the process.

Wayne wasn't sure if the man firing noticed the whole bullet-repel phenomenon, so he fell to the floor as if he'd been vitally hit. His arm flopped to his side as a ploy to go for the knife secured there.

When the clone bent over him, Wayne locked onto his vibration, transmitted it to Wylie, and thrust his knife into his clone's sternum.

Wayne felt the man's soft tissue rip and the blade grind against the bone. His cloned brother made a gurgling sound as he stiffened. As the knife tip sliced through vital organs, on the way to his heart, arterial blood spilled onto the twin beneath him. Slowly, the man slumped to the floor.

After retrieving the clone frequencies from Wayne, Wylie prepared to do some hunting of his own. He strapped some military-grade knives to his thighs, slung a bandolier with grenades over his shoulder, and strapped a gun to his hip. He tucked a smaller handgun into his lower back. Then he made his way to the last doctor on his agenda.

PRESENT DAY: Dr. Bellamy James

Bellamy James paced within the confines of his home. He knew about the breach of security at the offices of Dr. Turner because One called it in.

Three, a cloned soldier assigned to protect him asked, "Dr. James, do you want us to remain by you or help capture Wylie?"

Bellamy replied, "I want both."

The military man said, "Roger. I assume you want him to come to us?"

"Hell, I don't know!" said the doctor, raking his hand through his hair. "You have the military mind. What do you think?"

The clone replied, "We have a lock on his current location. All we need to do is show up. It may take all three of us to contain him, though. He's eliminated two of us already."

"Is that your recommendation?" asked the doctor.

"Yes." the man replied. "But we need to go now if we want to beat the police on-site and confront the target."

A second soldier said, "There's no telling what kind of fire power he'll bring if he comes here, sir."

"I guess go," Dr. James said. "I'm scared to be here alone, but if your chances are better there, then go."

As soon as they were gone, Bellamy began pacing rapidly. He kept glancing at his phone every few moments. Finally, he sighed.

"I'm driving myself insane," he muttered. "I need to calm down." He raked his fingers through his hair.

The doctor forced himself to sit and take slow, rhythmic breaths for a few minutes. Just when he had a semblance of steadiness, he imagined hearing footsteps. His heart caught in his throat, and he jumped to his feet when a soft tone sounded near him. It was a voice he'd hoped to never hear again.

"We meet again, Doctor." Wylie said with a low chuckle.

"W-Wylie?" asked Dr. James. He looked around but saw nothing.

"Were you expecting someone else?" Suddenly, a man appeared out of a ripple in the air.

"N - No..."

Wylie smiled and said, "Oh, that's right. You're trying to terminate me with brother clones, aren't you?"

Dr. James didn't respond.

"We have unfinished business." Wylie stated.

"Wylie... you know I have nothing against you. We didn't know you'd, well, you'd reincarnate in your entirety."

"Tell me where the data is." The soldier's voice was cold and harsh.

"Isn't life a better option than being on death row? Or worse? I don't understand, Wylie. Why?" Dr. James said, ignoring the command.

"I will not die repeatedly for you, Doctor. I want my own life."

"B – but," stammered Bellamy, "You're... you're not... safe for society."

Wylie grinned and gave a small shrug. "I may have learned my lesson."

"May have?" echoed Dr. James in shock. He took a step and exclaimed, "My dear God, you've eaten the hearts of your victims!"

"They were guilty," Wylie stated simply. He raised a shoulder and said, "They aren't the innocents of society. They knew exactly what they were doing."

"That's not how the world works, Wylie. You can't decide your own justice!"

Wylie lifted a suggestive brow.

"Haven't you learned that by now?" asked Dr. James, ignoring Wylie's silent accusation. The doctor took a couple of steadying breaths.

"Let's say we give you your freedom. Will that work?" His eyes begged him to agree. "Will you put a stop to this and work for us?"

"No, I'm afraid not, Doctor," Wylie said. "I'm still a target, and it would be stupid to trust you."

"But you'll be a target if you do this," reasoned Dr. James.

"Oh, really? I have news for you, Dr. James. I've got a plan that might just work."

"How?" asked the perplexed doctor. "You're state-of-the-art, yes, but there're devices out there even more technologically advanced than you. The Army will stop at nothing to get you back."

The cloned man replied, "Not if I'm dead."

"Why would you do that, Wylie?" asked the doctor. "Why all this if you intend to die?"

"Oh," Wylie laughed. "Death isn't permanent in my world," he said. "You know that."

The chilly words caused fear to electrify the doctor's spine.

"Is that why you want the data?" asked Dr. James.

"No," said Wylie slowly. "I want the data so that I have it and no one else does. I don't want this experiment repeated by those who know nothing."

"So… *you* would repeat it?" Bellamy gasped.

A slow smile formed on the clone's face. "Good doctor, I already have."

The doctor sucked in a sharp breath. His green eyes widened behind his glasses. "What?" he breathed. "What do you mean?"

"I've made my own clone," Wylie said. "And you could say we're identical in every way." He laughed at the doctor's whitening face.

"I – I must be missing something. You don't want anyone to repeat the experiment, but you've already done it yourself? This doesn't make any sense."

Wylie shrugged.

"You don't need to understand what's up here in my brain," said Wylie and tapped his head. "All I care about is getting the data."

He took a step closer and put a hand on the doctor's arm.

225

"There must be something else you want, Wylie! If I give you the data, will you let me live?"

"That," said Wylie, "I cannot do. I know you have a heart, Doctor, but unfortunately, I want it. That's the only other thing I desire."

"No, please! Wylie, I'll do what you want! I'll forget everything and set you free!" begged the doctor. "Please, have mercy!"

"If you give me the data, I won't make you suffer," Wylie offered. "I, too, have a heart."

The doctor nearly collapsed in fear, but Wylie pulled him back to his feet.

"Look," Wylie said reassuringly. "I'll let you in on a little secret. Your Yellow Charge has healed us from needing revenge."

Bellamy looked up sharply into cold brown eyes. "W – what?"

"Don't get your hopes up. This still won't end well for you, but I want to let you know that some of what you've researched is actually very good, powerful medicine. Yellow Charge works miracles, more deep and powerful ones than even you can fathom.

"There's also another part of your little experiment that worked very well. This brain you gave us, you know, the mission-driven one? Well, we *will* finish what we've started, but I thought I'd give you some solace by knowing that I actually won't be eating your heart."

<>< ><><><>

When Wylie finished, he went to the clone lab. He broke into the secured facility without the alarm system activating. It was child's play, really, to gather the stash of Yellow Charge from the EPDP, even in the encrypted and reinforced safe. He loaded up the cases of pills and the stolen laptop. Then, Wylie chose the most developed clones and punched in the activation frequencies.

"Wayne, get ready. Take a Yellow Charge. I'm going to activate another few of us, so I'll have help moving more of the clone population out of here. Then I'll send one of them back in to blow up the lab."

"Don't forget to set aside a clone to take the fall for us as proof of your death."

"Copy that. I'll make sure it's one without the detonation code while I take the future recruits to the bunker."

"Copy and out."

PRESENT DAY: Detectives Jewels and Joe

Jewels was asleep when the sound of explosions awoke her. In an instant, she was in her slacks, shirt, and jacket, strapping on her Glock. She called her partner from the car.

"Hello?" Joe's voice was sleepy.

227

"Joe! Did you hear that explosion?"

"Yeah, it came from Dr. James's place on the base," Joe replied. "I'm headed over there now."

"My God. Okay, I'll meet you there."

When the partners rolled up, they parked side by side and got out of their vehicles. The place was burning. They watched firefighters as they contained part of the blaze, but it wasn't safe for any to go in.

"It's going to take forever to dig all that debris away," Joe said. He shook his head.

"Yes, that's true. I'm going to guess Dr. James is in there somewhere." Jewel's shoulders were slumped.

"This was obviously intentional, so I'd say you're right," Joe agreed.

Just then, a call came over the radio.

"Officers needed. Dispatch to available officers. Shots fired, man down. Counseling building at address..."

"We're on it," said Joe, reaching in the patrol window to speak into the receiver.

"That's Dr. Turner's address," Jewels said.

"Yes, unfortunately, I'm sure the man down is him." Joe's expression was grim as he jerked open the patrol car.

"All the targets were taken out in one night," Jewels took in a shaky breath as she slid into the passenger seat. "I just hope he didn't do his usual. I don't think I can stomach another signature performance of his."

Joe nodded solemnly. "Me, either."

He turned on the lights and pressed the accelerator.

Other police and rescue vehicles arrived at the same time. A few crime scene analysts were already inside. Officer Burns was guarding the door.

"Is it as bad of a scene as the others?" Jewels asked tentatively. She was afraid of the answer.

"He was a busy boy tonight," confirmed Burns, "but at least he didn't have time to do his normal... art this time. The scene is bad, no doubt, but he wasn't, ah, decorative. He did remove the heart but didn't smear blood over the entire place."

"That's something, I guess," Jewels said, somewhat relieved.

The detectives walked into the office. Jewels had to cover her mouth. She thought she'd mentally prepared herself to see someone she knew as a victim.

"Oh, God. This is just... awful!" She coughed a few times and turned her face away to grab a couple of breaths. "He was so healthy and *alive*, just yesterday."

"Jewels, I'll handle this if you want," Joe's concern was etched in his face and reflected in his hazel eyes. He suggested, "Why don't you wait outside?"

"I'd feel bad doing that to you," she said, coughing a few more times. "The scene isn't as bad as his others, but it's just... it's just we actually met and talked with him. Just the other day..."

"There's not much to do. We'll leave it up to the forensic team. Go on. I'll be there soon."

Jewels left, coughing. She retched once and hurried from the room.

PRESENT DAY: Wylie and Wayne

In a moment of rest after all the evening's activities, the two clones of the same soul stood proudly in the bunker.

"There, that should do it," Wylie said to Wayne. "We've got all the clones unloaded and the entire amount of Yellow Charge from the lab."

"Do you want to accumulate the rest of the Yellow Charge?" Wayne asked.

"Affirmative. We need all that's been in production along with the data, but we need it quickly. As far as the science community knows, I'm dead now. All they have to do is dig my body out of the lab."

Wayne offered, "I'll go and pay Montrose a visit."

"Activate Chameleon," his soul brother suggested. "We need to keep it on at all times for a while."

"Roger."

"I'll stay here to instruct our newest brothers."

Wayne nodded and then was gone.

Wayne drove to Dr. Montrose's neighborhood. The tricky part now would be isolating the doctor. The man lived in a gated community. The good news, at least, was that the houses were not close to one another.

Wayne locked the vehicle in a secure location, and stealthily climbed over the fence guarding the district. Again, he had no issues entering the modern, peak-styled home. The security system offered the smallest of challenges.

Dr. Montrose was sleeping next to a pretty blonde in their king-sized bed. There were two children, each in their own rooms, down the hall. Wayne had no intention of killing anyone this time. He simply wanted the data.

Wayne took the water bottle next to the bed and let a few drips splash onto Montrose's face. The man rubbed his cheek, felt the water, then sat up and looked around. He didn't see The Chameleon standing beside him, so he stumbled sleepily into the bathroom. When Montrose shut the door, Wayne materialized behind him.

"Don't say a word," Wayne hissed.

Montrose paled and grabbed the counter in fright.

"I'm not here to kill you unless..." the clone said suggestively.

"Anything! Anything!" the doctor answered in a fearful whisper. "You must be..."

"I want the data on Yellow Charge. All of it."

"Uh, I have some here, but most of it is at the lab."

"Show me what's here," Wayne ordered.

Montrose slipped into a robe and quietly walked downstairs. He unlocked a large room stylishly equipped with quality office furniture. The cherry desk was enormous. Montrose sat behind it and rummaged for a key. He unlocked the safe and handed him hard copies along with drives containing the information.

"Now, the computer," Wayne announced. "Destroy the data. Every backed-up file."

Immediately, Dr. Montrose complied. Wayne pulled out the laptop and watched him do the same on the processor.

"Is that all?" The soldier asked. "You have no hard copies?" He's already obtained the capsules from the lab, but the doctor wasn't privy to that information.

"Y-yes," Montrose said. "Th – that's all that's here."

"You're sure? If I come back to pay you a visit, I won't be so… charming."

"It's all of it, I swear!" Dr. Montrose confirmed. "Th – there's some at the lab," he reminded, "but otherwise, you got it all. That laptop from the office is the only one that held the Yellow Charge information. Just don't hurt me or my family! Please!"

"You'll live, *this time*," Wayne said, "but I don't ever want to hear of you working on something like this again. Not for the military, anyway. If you wanted to modify this into a cure-all pill for the medical community, then that's one thing, but not for the military. Understand?"

Wayne loomed menacingly over his captive.

"Y-yes, sir!" Dr. Montrose cried, "I swear!"

"Good. If the Army comes to you, you know nothing."

"I – I understand. You were never here. Thank you... for allowing me my life."

"Be glad you weren't a part of the crew that tried to dictate my future."

Montrose nodded.

"If you're ever approached by the woman at the Disease Center, you may help her discover medical cures, but never again for the military."

"Uh, Dr. Taylor?"

"Yes. She has wholesome intentions. No one else." Wylie leveled a hard stare. The slender man seemed to shrink.

"I understand. Completely."

"Good."

With that, The Chameleon destroyed the computers completely and disappeared without a trace, data in-tow.

There was a frantic call from Dr. Montrose on Jewels's cell.

"You said to contact you if I wanted to talk?" The man was speaking rapidly, and his voice sounded shaky.

"Yes, of course, Dr. Montrose. Please, calm down," Jewels said into the phone. She tried to soothe him with her tone.

Joe was busy turning the car to face the direction of the doctor's home.

He pleaded, "Please, hurry! My family and I are scared."

"We're doing our best. My guess, though," Jewels said, "is that you're safe. You wouldn't have been able to call if this guy didn't want you to."

"That's true, but it doesn't make our terror any less real," he replied.

"I'm sorry, Doctor. I'm not trying to downplay your feelings. That was meant to reassure you," Jewels placated. "I'll stay on the phone with you until we arrive."

"Thank you, Detective," Dr. Montrose said, sounding relieved. "It means more than I can say."

Jewels continued to talk to the doctor until they pulled into his drive.

"We're here," she said. Jewels hung up the phone and pulled out her nine-millimeter. Joe pulled his out after parking the vehicle.

"Wow, would you look at this home," breathed Jewels.

An enormous home, made of gray stone and rose-hued brick, rose majestically from the acreage. There was an elaborate smoke-colored archway guarding the door and framing the attached multi-car garage. It contained many peaked sentries. The structure reminded Jewels of a castle. It was just missing the moat.

"Ridiculous, if you ask me. Why does any normal family need a household this big?" Joe asked.

"It's a beauty," Jewels said.

Joe grunted a response.

They knocked on the door, and immediately, Dr. Montrose ushered them in.

"You believe the 'Eat Your Heart Out' Killer was here?" Joe asked.

Jewels shot him a look. Her brows .

"Ummm - mm," Dr. Montrose said.

"You don't want to say?" Jewels asked. She paused for a moment then said, "I thought you wanted to talk."

The man nodded. "I - I do. But this can't get out. I was told, in no uncertain terms, that I can't admit I was visited … at least to the Army. I just hope he doesn't come back because you're here. I - I just didn't know what else to do."

"What makes you believe it was him?" Jewels asked. "I mean, to date, no one has ever survived when he's paid a personal visit."

"I just know," Dr. Montrose said evasively. He was white as a sheet and his eyes seemed triple their normal size.

"Well, what did he want? Did he take data from you?" Joe asked. He did his best to sound friendly rather than impatient.

"Yes, he did. Confidential military data," Dr. Montrose admitted, "He said if I gave it all to him, he wouldn't kill me."

"I would've done the same thing," Jewels said, trying to console him.

"The Army is going to come down on me, though," the doctor said miserably. His shoulders slumped in defeat. "And I can't tell them what happened to the data. What am I ever going to do?"

"Who would you rather be mad at you? Think of it that way." Joe suggested. He patted the doctor's shoulder awkwardly.

"You don't understand." Dr. Montrose shook his head emphatically.

"Probably not since most of the stuff you can't tell us," Joe agreed.

"I'm so sorry," said the nearly tearful doctor. "I - I can't, or I would. Th-thank you so much for coming."

PRESENT DAY: Wylie

Wylie/Wayne smiled. He was incredibly happy about the doctor's call to the detectives. His emotions surged when he saw Jewels step out of the car. It was something more than mere elation. He even felt a spark... elsewhere. The Chameleon felt his brow muscles lift in surprise.

Wayne felt Jewels had to see his progress from the beginning until now. Maybe, eventually, he'd have the courage to meet her face to face.

He stood beside the pretty brunette while she talked with Montrose. Once, he even ran a finger lightly down her arm. It was hard not to chuckle when she scratched the spot near her elbow.

PRESENT DAY: Detectives Jewels and Joe

Joe and Jewels sat at her desk when they arrived back at the station.

"Can you believe it?" Jewels asked. She leaned back in her chair. Her eyes still widened with surprise.

"I know, right? A survivor? Is he growing compassionate?" Joe asked.

"He certainly is breaking chains. We know he must have been a military experiment who was striking back at those he held responsible," Jewels said.

"The only good thing is that he doesn't seem to want to attack anyone not associated with his case," Joe said.

"True, but one can't trust that he won't break those boundaries and someday strike a civilian," Jewels pointed out.

"Granted. I will say, he's seemed to mellow with each murder. Most of our serials tend to grow more violent with each act."

"Yes, but this appeared to be revenge killings. You know the guy had to have been experimented on unmercifully for him to be this angry," Jewels stated.

"I agree. Well, except for the Turner girl. She shouldn't have been a target." Joe said thoughtfully. "I would love to know what all the data he's gathering has to do with his case. I mean, were they running World War II experiments on him like Mengele? Were they injecting him with illnesses and treating it with cryogenics? I would love to be a fly on the wall." Joe's eyes reflected his enthusiastic curiosity which contradicted his expression of thorough disgust.

"I think the same," Jewels said with a nod.

The rest of the day was spent studying the murder board and the rest of the collected data. Nothing made sense considering the connections they were trying to make.

"I wish we could analyze this chip," Jewels said, fingering the baggie.

"We can, but I want to find a trusted source." Joe said.

At that time, a call came from the front desk via intercom. "Um, detectives, you have a visitor."

"Okay. Show him into the interrogation room," Jewels responded. She looked up at Joe. He, too, wore an expression of concern. It was just too close to the exposure of the chip to not be suspicious.

When the partners walked into the room, they were shocked. A very distinguished general sat at the green metal table with his hands folded on top. He wore military dress greens, and many metals shone from the left side of his chest. Four stars decorated the top of both shoulders, and on his left arm, one could see a yellow ranger badge above an airborne patch. Below the two, his division insignia was depicted.

Two other high-ranking men stood behind him. They were like statutes, both alike in their stance. Their feet were apart, and their hands were clasped behind their backs. They did not move when the detectives walked in.

When the high-ranking officer stood, the detectives noted the general was a big, sturdy man, a few inches above six foot. He had a thick but muscular girth, much like a powerlifter. His tiny, mean-looking eyes perched over a smallish nose and thick, firm lips. His complexion was slightly ruddy.

The full force of his focus was on them, and his presence filled the room.

"H-hello, General…?" Joe asked.

"General Hawkins." The man's voice was clipped.

"To what do we owe this honor?" Jewels asked, recovering. Her eyes darted to her partner.

"I won't beat around the bush," he stated crisply. "I need the chip."

"What chip?" Jewels asked.

"The one you received from our man." He turned beady eyes to stare at her.

"That's part of a police investigation," Joe said.

The general's narrowed stare turned to Joe. "That's bullshit. This is a top-secret military operation. You do *not* have the clearance to be in possession of this chip."

"I received it, personally," Jewels said. "If it's so top-secret, respectfully sir, then how did it randomly appear in my purse?"

"We have a rogue soldier who is obviously not following orders," the general replied gruffly.

"Have you experimented on this man, General?" asked Joe. He wanted to show he wasn't intimidated.

The general's face hardened with that insinuation. His thick lips tightened and turned white.

"This is a highly confidential matter. All information related to this case is also strictly classified. You don't have access, detectives," The general rose to his full heights. "Now, if you'll hand over the chip and any data you've collected, I'd greatly appreciate it."

"No offense meant, General, but do you have any papers stating that we need to give our collected evidence on this case to you?" Joe asked.

The general's face puffed up and reddened to a darker hue. He took in a visible breath and released it before replying. "No, detectives. As a general, my orders are approved by the United States president. I am not required to provide you with a written directive. Now," he huffed angrily, "hand me my stuff, and I'm out."

"What a pleasant man," Jewels noted after the general had taken his leave.

"My thoughts precisely but with more expletives," Joe agreed.

"I guess we're officially off the case now," Jewels said.

"It looks that way."

Both detectives returned to Jewel's desk. Like synchronized swimmers, they sunk into chairs wearily.

"I'm relieved but at the same time, pissed. I hate having something we've worked so hard on taken away," Jewels finally admitted.

"I feel you," Joe said with a sigh. He rubbed the top of his bald head briefly. "Same here."

"It was just a matter of time, though," Jewel said, stating the obvious.

"With so much military involvement, I agree," Joe said. "It's disheartening they can rip apart the laws the rest of us are required to follow. It makes me sick."

"Me, too." Jewels paused in thoughtful consideration. "I wonder what happened to that guy."

"Eat Your Heart Out?"

"Yes." Jewel's eyes lost focus momentarily as she pondered.

"The news report said they found his body at the lab," Joe stated at last. "I guess he was killed in the explosion."

"Oh," Jewels said.

"I just heard it over the scanner. They're saying a possible suicide to take out the rest of the experiments."

"Really? That doesn't follow his M.O." said Jewels.

"Agreed. Seems a bit fishy, but we've got to buy in." Joe shrugged. He sighed, weaved his fingers behind his head, and leaned back in his chair.

"I guess so," Jewels said slowly. "Just for the record, though, I don't believe it's true."

Joe laughed. "Me, either."

Jewels waited a few minutes before saying, "Well, at least now I won't have to impose on you anymore."

"Kaylee will be disappointed."

Jewels laughed, "We do have some dates coming up."

"Games and bowling, yes?"

Jewels nodded with a soft smile.

"You know, that *is* coming up. As in tomorrow night."

Jewels gasped softly. "So soon?"

"Didn't you once ask if we could do it after this case?" Joe laughed.

"Oh, alright. I really do need to learn how to have fun, *especially* after this case."

PRESENT DAY: Bowling alley

The bowling alley was packed. There were forty lanes with an arcade, a few pool tables, and an air hockey table. For virtual reality lovers, there was a war game against aliens.

The precinct reserved eight lanes for family and the staff. Jewels headed to lane six where Joe, Cara, and Kaylee stood.

"Jewels." Kaylee waved and walked towards her.

"Hi, Kaylee," Jewels smiled genuinely. "Hi, Joe, hi Cara."

Joe nodded with a smile.

"We're glad you're here," Cara said. "We'll have a good time."

Jewels put her purse down by Cara's and looked around. She saw Rodriguez, Walsh, Lars, and Burns on lane five. All young, no families yet. In the next few lanes were four family units, and more people were arriving from the precinct.

"Wow," Jewels breathed. "I didn't realize so many of us liked to bowl."

Joe laughed. "I have a feeling there's a lot of things we all like that you don't know about, young lady."

Cara nodded in agreement.

Jewels sighed. "I suppose you're right. I do need to get out more."

Cara said, "Come on. We'll get you a ball to use and pick up your shoes."

Jewels allowed herself to be led to colorful house balls. Cara said, "The color indicates the weight."

"What weight are you going to use?" Jewels asked.

"I'd say… ten pounds. It doesn't sound like much, but it's a lot of weight to hold with your fingers and swing. When you get used to it, then you can adjust."

"That sounds like good advice," Jewels said. She found a blue ball with a comfortable finger width for her hand.

Cara picked up a ball for herself, and Jewels followed her to the ball receiver for the teams.

"I got my ball already," Kaylee said. "Dad brought his."

"You have your own ball?" Jewels asked, looking up at Joe with a raised brow.

"If you bowl often at all, it's better if you own your ball. You can drill it to match your hand span exactly, go fingertip, which makes it hook more, or you can do all sorts of things to suit your style. Not so with a house ball."

"You can throw a ball with your fingertips?" Jewels asked with wide eyes.

Joe laughed. "You don't actually throw it with your fingertips, but it is easier to drop if you're not used to it," he said. "But some people actually bowl without using finger holes."

"Oh, okay," Jewels stated. "I didn't know this much went into the sport."

Cara smiled. "Oh, you know Joe. He's a good ole guy, but he is a bit competitive."

"I've got to keep up with the Joneses, you know. Besides, my team expects me to be good."

"You even bowl on a team?" Jewels asked. "How didn't I know this?"

"Hum," Joe said with a twinkle in his eye. "Probably because you're too busy working on cases."

"Point taken. Well, I suck, so you won't have any competition with me."

"We're here to have fun," Cara reminded.

"Oh, we'll have fun when I win," Joe said with a wink. His wife punched him playfully.

"We'll fit in together," Cara said to Jewels in a conspirator's whisper. "Let's just let him win, and we'll play for fun."

"You're not even going to try?" Joe snorted.

"I'll try to keep it on the lane," Jewels said. "Is that what you mean?"

Joe blew up his cheeks and let the air out slowly as he looked up.

Kaylee burst out laughing. "Oh, my goodness. This is going to be fun just watching you three."

The other group on lane five approached them. Jewels noticed the bright hair contrasts. Burns had mahogany hair and matching eyes, Lars's dusty blond with blue eyes, the standout redheaded Walsh, and Rodriguez's black nearly indigo blue hair.

Lars said, "You're bowling on our set of lanes. That's great! We'll have a good time." He held up a beer and took a swallow. He looked at Jewels and said, "Hey, good to see you here, Polten."

"Thanks, Lars," she said with a grin. "It's, uh, good to get out."

Walsh said, "These three don't bowl much." She waved at the three men standing next to her, "so I'll have to school them."

"Oh, you a bowler?" asked Joe. "Why aren't you in the league?"

"Well, I didn't want to intrude on the man party," she responded with a grin.

"Look us up next season," Joe said. "We need a good strong member if you can back up what you say." He winked at her. "Can your motorcycle mouth back up your tricycle ass?"

Walsh barked out a laugh. "It's a tricycle made by Harley."

"Dad!" Kaylee said. Cara just shook her head.

"We've got enough people to get this party started," Rodriguez said. "Wanna begin?"

"Sure. Why not?" Joe said. "If you're ready to get stomped."

Those who needed shoes got them from the attendant, and the lane lights came a few moments later.

"You bowling first, Rodriguez?" Joe asked.

"Nah, good bowlers bowl last."

Joe laughed. "Just checking."

"This first game is the trial run to see who earns anchor for the next game," Walsh said. "I'll let you have anchor now as a courtesy. You won't see that position again for the rest of the night."

"Pretty confident, aren't you?" Rodriguez joked back. "You're on."

"Dad, you are definitely anchor on our side," Kaylee said.

He snorted a response.

"If the best bowler bowls last, that means I need to go first," Jewels said.

"I'll bowl after you," Kaylee said.

"Sounds good, sweetie," Jewels said. She picked up her ball and approached the lane. She threw it, and it careened to the gutter.

"Well, at least you get another chance to get pins," Joe tried to suppress a smile.

She threw again, but this time, the ball crashed into the opposite gulley.

"Um, I'm sure you'll get some when you warm up, dear," Cara said.

Joe coughed into his hand.

"It's all good," Jewels said, but she could feel her cheeks warming a bit.

Kaylee got seven pins. Her mom followed with a spare, and Joe scored a strike.

"How did you get your ball to curve like that?" Jewels asked. "You looked like a professional."

Cara reached over and whispered, "Don't tell him that. It goes straight to his head."

Kaylee laughed.

"It's the fingertip I was telling you about. Sometimes it's harder to get spares, but it sure helps with pin action."

"All this bowling lingo," Jewels said. "It's a bit over my head."

"It'll all make sense if you stick with it," Joe said.

After three more balls, Jewels bowled a strike.

"Wow," Joe said. "Now remember what you did."

After a few more frames, Walsh and Joe were pulling ahead of the others in score. Rodriguez was close behind.

"After I warm up after a game, I'll kick your butt," Rodriguez said to Walsh. "I'm gonna laugh if the old man beats you."

"You should, because that means he'll be beating you, too. If you need to review the score, you're in third."

When they finished the first game, Kaylee asked, "Mom? Can we get some nachos and a drink or something?"

"Sure, sweetie. Get some popcorn, too." Kaylee could already hear the ribbing going on behind her.

"You ready to give up the anchor spot now, Rodriguez?" Walsh teased.

"Damn, I guess I am third. I challenge you to a rematch, though."

"Any time," Walsh said.

I guess I don't get a rematch because I'm that good," Joe said. He blew on his knuckles then rubbed them on his shirt with a wicked grin.

"Oh, my God. I'm going to have to get my boots because it's getting deep in here," Jewels said while shaking her head.

"You learn to ignore it after a while," Cara said.

Jewels laughed. "You know, this *is* a good time."

"We're so glad you're having fun," Cara responded. She put an arm around her in good nature.

Kaylee came back and handed the change to her mother. "The cashier said someone would bring it to our table when it's ready."

"Okay, Dear," her mother said.

"Hey, Jewels?" Kaylee asked.

"Yes?"

"Did you see that guy over there against the water fountain? I noticed that he keeps staring at you. He's kinda cute. You should go say hi."

"If he's been staring, that kinda creeps me out," Jewels said.

"Oh, come on. Go say hi," Kaylee said. "I would."

Jewels looked toward the fountain. "I, um, don't see anyone there?"

"Oh, well I bet he went in the bathroom," Kaylee said with a bit of disappointment. "Maybe you should go, too. I'll bet he'll have to get a drink or something if he's not in the men's room."

Cara agreed with a firm nod.

"Oh, alright. I'm just gonna say hi, and that's all."

Cara said, "And it wouldn't hurt to get his number."

When Jewel's head swiveled around to gape at her, Cara raised her shoulders slightly and stated innocently, "Um, you know... we might need an extra partner to play games with is all."

"Um, hum," Jewels said in an unbelieving tone. "Well, here goes." She turned her back to her friends and walked purposefully towards the women's room.

"Well, I might as well make it a real thing," she mumbled to herself. She decided to use the facilities. When she came out, indeed, an attractive man was getting a drink of water. He looked up at her when she exited the room.

"Oh, hello," she said.

"Hi." He stood up and smiled at her. It accentuated his masculine beauty. "How are you?"

"I'm fine," Jewels replied, hoping she didn't come across as awkward as she felt. She decided to get a drink as well and stood in line behind him.

The man moved aside. "I'm finished with my drink," he said with an amused twitch to his lips. He watched as she lowered her mouth to the water stream and drank. When she straightened, he asked, "You bowl here often?"

"Um, did you see me bowl?" she asked. She could feel the heat begin to rise from her cheeks again.

"I'm not going to lie. Yes, I've watched you for a few frames."

"Okay, then, what do you think after assessing my skill level?" she asked, embarrassed.

"I'm going to take a stab in the dark and guess... no."

She smiled. "No, but I'm expanding my horizons."

"Trying new things?"

"That's the plan," she said. "Do you bowl here often?"

"My plan is the same as yours. I'm trying new things."

"Nice," Jewels said. "I'm Jewels, by the way."

The man took her hand in his and held it for a few moments. Tingles raced up her arm.

The man said, "You can call me William."

Jewels looked up at him, and he released her hand. "Is that not your real name?"

"Oh, I'm a man of many names. That's the one I prefer right now."

"Oh, okay," Jewels said. She shot him a questioning look. "Well, um, *William*. It was very nice to meet you." Her eyes darted to her friends.

"Yes," he said. "I'm very pleased to make your acquaintance."

His intense brown eyes captured Jewels's attention again, consuming her. The sheer magnetic draw pulled unexpectedly at her.

She took an involuntary step back. Softly, she said, "I probably should be getting back."

"I'm sure I'll see you around," he replied. A suggested smile played about his mouth and seemed to soften his hard features.

Jewels took a few steps toward her friends and turned back to say something, but he was already gone.

Cara and Kaylee bombarded her as soon as she reached their table.

"Who was that?" Kaylee asked.

"Did you get his number?" Cara asked.

"Whoa, wait a second," Jewels said. "What, Kaylee? What do you mean, 'who was that'? Wasn't that who you sent me to meet?"

"No, that guy over there is," she said, pointing discreetly.

Jewels looked and saw an attractive guy playing a claw machine.

"He was really checking you out, but he put coins in that machine when he saw you talking to that other man."

"Way to go," Cara teased. "You have two guys interested without even trying."

Jewels sat down. She absently put a nacho in her mouth.

Joe walked up. "Everything okay, Jewels?" He wore a slightly concerned look.

"Everything is fine, dad. We're just trying to get her more adventurous in the man department. She could have gotten one guy's number already. Now she could get another's." Kaylee giggled.

Joe didn't pay his daughter any attention. He sat down across from Jewels and studied her features, trying to read her body language. "Jewels. Talk to me."

Cara and Kaylee quieted.

"Joe. It just hit me," Jewels said. "but I'm probably just overreacting."

"What?" Joe asked. "What just hit you? Is it because you're getting attention? It's perfectly normal for guys to hit on you."

"No, no. It's... not that. This guy, well..." She trailed off then turned to Kaylee and Cara. "Did that guy remind you of the military in any way?"

Kaylee said, "His haircut was definitely something an Army man would wear."

Cara said, "Now that you mention it, he had the posture of a guy with military training, but who knows for sure? Why? Are you more attracted to veterans or active soldiers?"

Joe's mouth opened slightly. "Jewels. Are you thinking what I think you're thinking?"

"It's hard not to let it cross my mind, Joe. Is it possible?"

Joe looked down at the table, suddenly stressed. Both hands rubbed over his bald head. He blew out air from his cheeks.

"What?" Cara and Kaylee asked in unison.

"Not now, ladies," Joe stressed. "This is very... we must be quiet." He glanced around at his fellow officers to make sure they weren't the center of attention.

"Dad, are you saying that man had something to do with your case?" Kaylee whispered. Her eyes were large pools of excitement in her face.

Joe looked up with stern intensity directed on his daughter; he didn't need to say another word.

"Jewels, are you sure this man is gone?" he asked.

"Yes, Joe. We spoke at the fountain, I took two steps, and turned back. It was like he disappeared. He wasn't threatening in any way... aside from the fact he made purposeful contact."

"Tell me what he looked like."

"He was about six foot, very fit, close military cut brown hair, and brown eyes."

"Did he identify himself?"

"Not really."

"What does that mean?"

"It means he didn't give me anything we could use. He said I could call him William. It sounded fishy immediately, so I asked him if that was his real name. He said he went by many names."

"Yeah, I can see that. The media called him one thing, his friends, another, then I'm sure the military called him something else, as well."

"What do we do, Joe? I feel like we should clear the area, but I'm sure he's long gone."

About that time, Lars asked, "You all up for another one? We're going to start soon."

"Give us just a few minutes," Joe said.

"Sure, bud. I'm sure you need time to recharge," Rodriguez said with a chuckle.

"Ha ha, you're quite funny, young man," Joe said with a forced laugh.

When the younger man returned to his table, Joe asked quietly, "You got your Glock?"

"Never leave home without it."

"We're going to step outside for a moment. We'll be right back," Joe called to the other team. Then he turned to his wife and daughter. "You ladies stay here."

Cara and Kaylee nodded somberly.

"Order us a beer, please," Joe added with a reassuring smile. "We'll be back."

"Um, Dad?" Kaylee called softly.

"Yes?"

She mouthed the words, "*be careful*."

"Of course, sweetheart."

Joe and Jewels pulled their guns discretely and cleared the parking lot. Then methodically, they returned inside and did the same as casually as they could.

"Did you see anything strange?" Cara asked when they finally returned.

"Not a thing," Joe said.

"We may have been totally overreacting," Jewels admitted. "This case has taken a lot out of both of us."

Cara and Kaylee nodded.

"Well, the first night out wasn't so relaxing," Jewels said and everyone at the table broke into laughter.

"You ready to bowl now?" Burns asked.

"Line 'er up," Joe said. He picked up his beer and took a long swallow.

Jewels picked up hers and took a healthy drink as well.

Cara stood and put a hand on each of their shoulders. She pulled them close, leaned forward, and put her face next to theirs. In a low tone, she asked, "Are you two sure you feel like staying? We can go if you'll feel better."

"No, no," Jewels said, shaking her head. "This just proves how much we... um, *I* need stress relief. The case is over, taken from our hands, so in essence, closed. It just goes to show how much we've been focused on it."

Jewels took another pull from her beer and said, "I need to learn to relax, and I'm not doing a very good job."

"You were doing great until I forced you to go say hi to a guy," Kaylee said miserably.

"Kaylee, babe, it isn't your fault," Jewels said. "I just have to learn to relax and let go. As you can see, it may take me baby steps. I promise."

"Sweetheart, you were just helping. It's okay," Joe said. "It came from us working too hard on a stressful case. You okay, now?"

Kaylee nodded.

Walsh called to their table, "Hey, you guys gonna bowl or what?"

Jewels grabbed her ball and stood on the approach. "Yeah, what's taking you so long?" she asked.

After bowling, The Combs family walked to the parking lot with Jewels.

"If you don't mind, I'd feel better if we walk you to your car," Joe said. The other two nodded.

"Of course, I don't mind," she said. When Jewels arrived at her car, she turned on her flashlight app and shone it around before entering. Right when the Combs trio were turning to go to their car, Jewels called them back. "Uh, Joe?"

Immediately, his alert face was peering in her door. "What is it, Jewels?" he asked. His voice was a little breathy.

"He *was* here. My car was locked, but somehow, he was here."

"How do you know?"

"Because of this," Jewels held up a baggie with a yellow capsule and a note neatly folded inside. "I've never seen it before, and it was laying in the middle of my seat."

"I know it's not procedure to see what it says, but I know we're not on his target radar," Joe said. "Let's read it."

"Agreed."

Jewels unsealed the Ziplock then carefully retrieved the letter. Slowly, she unfolded the note and read.

Detectives,

I know I've messed with your minds by involving you in this case, and for that, I apologize. You were diligent, and I know you would've eventually figured it all out had you been left in charge and in possession of the chip. You were on the correct trail though your focus was a bit skewed. I want to thank you for your meticulousness.

I've left you a present, another clue, if you will. Take it but tell no one actively involved with the government. If you mention to anyone that you received this letter, the especially important content will be confiscated from you as well and will be lost to the medical community. I also suggest you permanently destroy this letter after reading.

This pill is magic. Literally. Take it to a doctor. I suggest Dr. Taylor who you've spoken to. Have her analyze it. She will do what should be done. It's too powerful for civilian use, but the healing qualities will make you millionaires. If a doctor could market just the healing abilities, there'd be no need for health care again. Good luck.

By the way, Detective Polten, it was nice meeting you tonight. I regret that it couldn't have been under different circumstances. Farewell. You won't hear from me again.

"Well, I'll be damned!" said Joe. He scratched his head as he mused. "Jewels, can I bother you into staying one more night at the house? I think we need to discuss this."

"Sure, Joe. I'll follow you over there."

PRESENT DAY: Wylie, Wayne, and William

William arrived at the bunker. He was greeted by several active shadows of himself.

"That was exciting," he said. "Getting to meet Detective Polten was more of a ride than an assassination."

"*Yes, we've admired her for quite some time,*" his reflections said into his mind.

William sat. "I wish we could do more than meet her in person. I wish we could develop a relationship with her."

"*We all do,*" the collective thought together.

William stopped talking with words and joined in the telepathic conversation.

"*The more of us there are, the stranger this gets. It's like we're having a conversation with ourselves.*" This time, the collective laughed aloud.

"*Doesn't everyone talk to themselves?*" Wylie asked.

"*Not like this,*" Wayne said.

"*Hey,*" Wyatt said, "*Now that we've met the detective, we can get her out of our mind. Let's focus back on our mission.*"

Although no one wanted to forget Detective Polten, their soldier minds were determined to let nothing get in the way of their agenda.

PRESENT DAY: Detectives Jewels and Joe

I don't know whether to like this guy or hate him!" Joe said.

They were sitting at the kitchen table. Cara had made Kaylee prepare for bed to give them time to analyze the new finding.

"I agree! I mean, he brutally kills his victims and then plays with their bodies." Jewel's face waded up and reflected her disgust.

"Don't forget that he also eats their heart," Joe reminded.

"Gross. I *know*. I'd rather forget that part, but what a noble thing he's done," Jewels said, shaking her head.

When she noticed Joe's eyebrows raise, she explained, "He's impossible to figure out. A murderer who wants to save lives? And did you notice that he's changed since we've been on the case?"

"Jewels... I don't know if I'd quite call it changing. Yes, his murders did grow a little less violent, but they were still very violent. He didn't play with the bodies or eat the hearts out of his last few victims, but his murders were still high on the dysfunctional chart. And who knows? Maybe he didn't have time for his normal artwork."

"True, but any less violence is a good thing." She paused and said thoughtfully, "He said we were kind of close to the mark." Her voice grew a little louder, "I think he meant he was experimented on by that general and company. Maybe by the Technology of Tomorrow and The Disease Center as well."

"But we must have been off the mark a bit," Joe said. "He's still trying to redirect us."

"Um, I really don't know where. I mean, what else could it be?" Jewels laughed. "The Army surely didn't clone a criminal or anything."

Joe joined in on her laughter. "God, I'd hope not."

"Wouldn't that be insane?" Jewels snorted and then laughed a little harder with embarrassment.

The next morning, after several bad cups of coffee at her worn desk, Jewels walked to Joe's work area. She said, "I'm going to call Dr. Taylor in a few minutes. Do you think we should have her come in?"

"No," Joe said. "It's obvious our friend has been watching us. If he has, you can bet that the general is now, too."

Jewels said, "Do you really think so? It seems like the whole ordeal is over to the rest of the world by what the papers reported – 'Found: incinerated body of unidentified man who is suspected Eat Your Heart Out Killer' and all... Personally, I think that must have been what our killer wanted. I think we're the only ones who may know he's still about."

Joe said, "Yeah, us and Montrose." He paused. "Although that may be true, we still need to keep it on the down low. Let's meet somewhere... like we can 'run into her' at lunch. Somewhere we can talk privately."

"Good point," Jewels agreed thoughtfully. "Any recommendations?"

"Hum. Let me think about it," Joe said.

"Well, I'm going to give her a call. Maybe she'll have some ideas."

Jewels walked back to her desk and rummaged around for the doctor's phone number. A few minutes later, the phone was ringing.

"Dr. Marla Taylor speaking."

"Hello, doctor. It's Detective Polten. Do you have a moment?"

After a pause, the doctor's husky voice said, "Yes."

"We have something of great importance we'd like to discuss with you. You will find it very... motivating. Is there a place we can meet? I would like it to look... coincidental and not planned."

"Oh... kay," Dr. Taylor said. "Well, I guess we could meet at a little tearoom down the street from The Disease Center. Would that work?"

"Well," said Jewels, "how much privacy does it offer? We'd like to talk but not be overheard."

"It's a house that was converted into a tearoom. There is a private room I usually eat in. I sometimes take a file to work on while there."

"Yes, I believe that would be great. Thank you. Say about 11:30 today?"

"Yes. I'll call to make a reservation. I'll see you there."

"Thank you, doctor."

When she got off the phone, Jewels turned to Joe who was standing expectantly by her desk.

"What do you think about a froo froo woman eatery for lunch?" she grinned broadly. "I don't mind, but I wasn't sure what you'd think." Before he could answer, she added, "Tearoom food is actually very delicious."

"Sure, why not?" Joe asked. "I can handle it for a good cause." He grinned and patted his stomach.

"Have you eaten at tea rooms before?" Jewels asked suspiciously. She raised a brow as she peered up at him.

Joe laughed. "You're good, detective. Who trained you?" He waited a beat before adding, "I'll let you in on a little secret." He leaned down close to her ear and whispered, "I have a wife and daughter."

"Ah, that makes sense." Jewels waited a beat before adding, "I want to leave in two hours."

"Okay. I'll be working right over there until then," Joe said pointing at his desk with a wink. Jewels nodded and turned back to her own pile of work to complete.

PRESENT DAY: Detectives Jewels and Joe with Dr. Marla Taylor

Joe parked in the cramped lot outside the charming tearoom. To all outward appearances, it looked like a light mauve house with white trim. Though small, the restaurant was immensely popular.

"Table for two?" the hostess asked.

"We're meeting a third," Joe said.

"Dr. Taylor? I believe she called for a reservation." Jewels added.

The woman's demeanor changed immediately. "How lovely. We just love her here. Please, follow me."

A few patrons still waiting to be seated shot looks of frustration at their backs.

The hostess said, "Dr. Taylor isn't here yet, but she's usually prompt. I'm sure you'll only have to wait a few minutes."

"Thank you," Jewels said.

"I'll be back with your waters and menus," she returned.

"Thank you," Joe said.

Jewels looked at their attire and said softly, "At least we're not as conspicuous."

"Because we're in civilian clothes?" Joe asked.

"Exactly. It's not like we wear uniforms daily, but this really is casual wear." Jewels pointed out. "I don't think anyone out there guessed we're cops."

"I agree." Joe looked down at his jeans and button-down plaid. He ran a hand down the front of the shirt, hoping to smooth out the slight bit of wrinkling.

"You look nice. I don't think it's too casual," Jewels said. "You're more dressed up than I am."

"I wouldn't go that far. You look lovely, Jewels."

Jewels wore a nice sleeveless shirt of whispering green that would serve either purpose: Casual or dress. She wore it with jeans.

"Thanks," she said.

The stewardess appeared with their drinks. She was followed by Dr. Taylor. They smiled and stood while Dr. Taylor took her seat. Then, they sat as well.

The stewardess handed them menus and told them their server would be with them shortly. After she left, the trio began conversing.

"This is quite a place you've got here," Jewels said. "It's really a delightful spot to work and eat your lunch."

"I quite enjoy it," Dr. Taylor said.

"Thank you so much for agreeing to meet us today," Jewels said.

"It's nice to see you again, detectives. To what do I deserve this honor? I was really surprised to hear from you this morning. I, um, thought this case was closed," Dr.

Taylor said. She crossed her legs and folded her hands in her lap.

"Oh, it is," Joe agreed, "but we still have run into some remarkably interesting information. We know you'll love our discovery as well."

"But there's a catch," Jewels said. "If we give you this… thing we have, you cannot say who you got it from. You cannot say anything that portrays it has to do with the case."

"Should I be concerned?" The doctor's wide hazel eyes looked a little startled. "It sounds like something I may need to stay away from."

"Well, we feel we can trust you, and so does someone else," Joe said. "Someone I think we should not take lightly."

Marla swallowed. "Shall I ask?"

"I think you probably already have guessed," Jewels said. "Our friend is not dead, but we still cannot work on the case. A general came with orders for us to relinquish our accumulated data. Case closed for our department."

"I, um, don't understand. The case is closed but you're still working on it?" the doctor asked.

"Yes," Jewels said. "Not officially, of course."

The waitress appeared in the doorway. "Do you all still need a few more minutes to decide?" she asked.

"Yes, please," said Dr. Taylor. "Give us ten."

The waitress nodded and disappeared.

Joe said, "Let's get our order in before we continue."

"Good idea," Jewels nodded. "Otherwise, we'll never get to lunch."

Ten minutes later, the waitress flashed through, capped waters, and brought ordered drinks. She scribbled each order on her pad and left.

"Look," Jewels said, taking a sip from her strawberry lemonade, "I was given another bit of data from our man. Whether I wanted it or not, he gave it to me directly. He also gave us an explanation via note. I'm going to read it to you. After that, I'll destroy it. I don't want to disregard a directive from this guy."

The doctor's breath caught in her throat. "He... he mentioned me in the letter?"

Joe nodded. Jewels pulled the letter from her pocket, unfolded it, and read it quietly.

Marla picked up her water, but her hands shook so much that water sloshed a bit over the sides. She replaced the glass on the table. "So, um, this killer gave you a chip the government confiscated?" she asked.

"Yes. The general also took notes we retrieved from a crime scene from Dr. Turner. No, we don't know what they said. They were basically encrypted by all the medical jargon."

"I wonder if..." the doctor began. She tried for another drink.

"If?" Joe prompted.

"Remember, I told you I found evidence of a big cure but too much was missing to put together? All the essential data was gone. It was impossible to recreate the experimental drug even with the documentations of clients walking away, completely in remission?" Marla said.

"Yes, of course," Joe said.

"I can't help but wonder if this is what he's given you to give to me. But why would a killer care? It really doesn't make much sense. And it's really quite disturbing that he knows we talked. How would he know that?" The doctor took another nervous sip of her water.

"Since we are no longer on the case, I'll tell you our theory," Jewels said. "I can't stress enough how confidential this is."

Joe added, "Although our friend is helping us to figure out what's going on, he is certainly not someone I trust. I'm thankful that he hasn't targeted us, but it's obvious that he's watched us all."

"So, in other words, we don't want to do anything to set him off and make him put us on his list," Jewels clarified.

"Understood. He's the unstable variable."

The detectives nodded as one.

"We don't know how he moves the way he does," Jewels said. "He seems to be undetectable, or the Army or whomever would have stopped all this long ago. Our advice is to just walk a tight line. He did mention you, so just so you're aware..."

"He's probably watching you closely, too," Joe said. "We aren't trying to scare you, but you should keep that in the back of your mind."

"Of course. That makes me nervous as hell, but there's not much I can do about it. I'll be very discrete and keep you two in the loop with what I find out," Marla said.

"Thank you," Jewels said with sincerity.

Their meals arrived, and they ate in the semi-comfortable, fragile bonds of an alliance.

PRESENT DAY: Reverend John

The day was clear, and a pleasant breeze was cooling down the warm temperatures of the afternoon. Reverend John decided a walk would be just the thing before his evening sessions of the Twelve-Step Program.

The preacher truly cared about helping troubled souls. He led the recovery program for those on probation five days a week and visited the penitentiary daily. There, he led another twelve- step program as well as visited and/or counseled death row inmates.

Walks cleared his mind of the negativity he encountered daily. He whistled a tune and appreciated the beauty around him. The vibrant blue sky, the puffy wisps of white clouds, the green and golden grasses and the colorful splashes of late summer flowers. One was lucky to be alive.

As John walked and felt the gratitude strum through him, he noticed the sound of falling footsteps approaching. He glanced over his shoulder and saw a very fit looking man walking rapidly toward him. He was focused and staring directly at him.

John looked around and noticed others out for an afternoon stroll as well. He released a drawn-out breath then slowed down. He moved to the edge of the sidewalk and watched the stranger's approach. It was only a few moments until the man was beside him.

"Hello, Reverend John," the man said, making direct eye contact.

"Hello, um...?" John fumbled for the words to greet the stranger. Finally, he asked, "I'm sorry, but have we met?"

"Sort of. My name is Wylie. I just wanted to tell you thank you for what you do, Reverend."

"Oh? Well, thank *you*, young man. I appreciate that. Sometimes, you need a little thanks."

"Hard day?"

"Just a lot on my mind. My life's mission is to help those who have trouble helping themselves, and sometimes it just lays heavily on me." John studied the man more closely. "Have you visited one of the programs I sponsor? I'm so sorry that I don't recognize you. I assure you, this isn't my normal practice."

"It's okay, Reverend. I looked a lot different the last time we met."

"Have you lost a lot of weight? Cleaned up your act?"

The stranger offered a little laugh. "No, neither, but I'm actually a completely different person. You wouldn't believe me if I told you."

"You've certainly piqued my interest. Wylie, did you say?" John asked. He rubbed his jaw gently back and forth while he tried to place the name. "Where was it I met you?"

The man smiled. "I said you won't believe me if I tell you."

"You must want me to know, I'll guess?" The preacher smiled, hoping to reassure the man.

"I was on death row."

John's mouth dropped open and his eyes widened momentarily before he could recover.

"How can this be so?"

"I'll tell you a little tale," Wylie began. "My name was once Wright."

John drew in a breath and held it. His eyes were incredulous. "Are you a relative? How do you know Wright? I didn't think he... had any family left."

"Do you want to continue walking while we talk?" Wylie asked. "I know you've got an open mind, but Rev, what I'm about to tell you may shake you to the core."

The man of God looked around him again. He saw many out for strolls, so he nodded and resumed a nice steady pace.

"Do you remember the conversation we had before my execution?" Wylie asked.

John nodded. "Yes, I recall the conversation I had with Wright."

Wylie smiled. "That was me, Rev. Let me remind you about that conversation, and you can be the judge. I had a lot on my mind that day. I was worried about Karma and reincarnation. You told me that basically Christians didn't believe in it, but you educated me about different interpretations on the subjects and answered all my questions with an open mind."

The preacher's steps faltered. He stared at Wylie for a few moments. "How could you know that?"

"I told you, this is going to be hard for you, Rev. I didn't come back here to destroy the foundations of your beliefs, but rather, I came because you've helped me more than you know. You told me that anything is possible through God. Now, to be honest, I am still not sold on the whole big man concept, but I will say that I've truly changed. I no longer kill for revenge."

"Th - that's praiseworthy."

"I'd have said it wasn't possible," Wylie said. "You're a good man. Death row inmates really benefit from what you do, Rev."

John slowed, then stood quietly. He didn't know which of the many questions flooding his mind to ask.

"You okay?" the man asked.

"Y - yes. There're… so many questions."

"Rev, for your own safety, I can't tell you all. I just wanted to tell you thanks… and to validate what you do. You give hope, even when there's none. I never thought I could… or *would* change. You might call that a miracle where I'd call it science, but maybe it's a mixture of both. In the past, I *was* Wright. I am now Wylie, a changed man."

"Do… you … still want to…"

"Kill? I'm not going to answer that, Rev. If you need reassurance that you're safe from me; you are very safe. For what it's worth, I give you my word, *our* words, rather, that we will never hurt you."

"We?" The preacher swallowed hard.

Wylie didn't seem to notice John's last utterance. He continued, "I'm going to let you revisit and ponder your beliefs and come to your own conclusions because I really don't have the answers. Who knows what the answers really are?"

"We have knowledge in our souls that God provided us with," John said. "He's also given us the Bible as a guide."

"I thank you again, Rev," Wylie said. "You'll probably never see me again, but keep up the good work."

John wiped his forehead and squinted up in the late afternoon sun. When he glanced back at the stranger, Wylie was no longer there. The preacher did a slow three-sixty turn, searching for the man's silhouette, but somehow, he'd completely disappeared.

PRESENT DAY: General Hawkins

General Hawkins sat heavily in his recliner. He was extremely agitated. It was the same, night after night. He sat and drank himself into a stupor as he rehashed the phases of the experiment and pondered what he could have done differently.

He raged that nothing had gone according to plan. Now all the doctors he'd collaborated with were dead, and he had no data except for what was left on the confiscated chip and notes.

The general lifted a hefty shot glass filled with scotch and threw it in the back of his throat in one swift movement. He swallowed with a grimace. He'd had several already, and finally, it was beginning to numb his misery. The depression had been pressing against his psyche for some time, and he was ready to get some relief. He poured yet another as he continued reflecting on his failure.

It had taken a lifetime to achieve the progress he had. Hell, they'd had a successful living clone. He was a dream-come-true for the military, but the other possibilities for clones were endless. He could have been a very wealthy man, and now, here he sat in a chair that had seen better days. He'd spent all his life's savings on this investment. He had nothing. He sighed. At least he had enough left on his pension to limp along.

Maybe he could sell his idea to a research university who would have time to redevelop the data. More than likely, though, he couldn't relinquish control. He'd probably request a transfer to the U.S. Army Combat Capabilities Development Command (DEVCOM) Army Research Laboratory and start all over again. He'd wanted all the glory, but now, he'd have to share. He sighed. He knew that it would take years, and he'd end up letting the next upcoming officer take over before the project was seen to fruition. The lucky winner would be eons ahead of where Hawkins had been when he started. *Yes, that's what he would do*, he decided. It was the only way to piece together his pride... and finances.

The sensitive binocular-like vision from the collective zeroed in on the general. The unsuspecting man huffed angrily while sitting alone. Occasionally, he would slam down a large fist on the table or into his other hand, his lips would mutter strung-together profanities, and he'd pour another shot glass, and down it. It was nearly amusing.

The Wylie Collective knew it was an advantage that the officer believed him to be dead. There would be a time when Hawkins was a bit more comfortable than he was now. He'd become less cautious. When that day came, Wayne, Wylie, Wyatt, William, and the other W's would be waiting for him... for they had a score to settle.

If you liked this story, *A Killer, Revisited,* I would greatly appreciate a positive review. The following site(s), especially Goodreads, would be very helpful. Thank you. **Sheri**

Goodreads
Powell's City of Books
Strand
Book Depository
Barnes and Noble
Walmart
Amazon
and more

Author Bio:

Sheri Chapman loves life and laughing, but you couldn't tell it by her writing. Although she writes historical romance, a lot of her work is suspense/thriller, supernatural, shape shifter, dark fiction, and a dab of horror.

Professional experience for Sheri includes teaching in Missouri Public schools. She recently retired (2020) with thirty years of experience. Now she splits her time between writing, Working with Trient Press, and working on her farmette. Sheri has chickens and a few Nigerian goats, but most of her non-writing time goes to raising exotic-colored fluffy Pomeranians.

On the personal front, Sheri is the mother of four beautiful daughters. She and their father enjoy spending time with each other, family, and friends. Aside from reading and writing, Sheri loves animals and being outdoors. She likes going for walks, fishing, scuba diving, kayaking, playing games, and watching movies. She is a big Harry Potter fan.

For those interested in Sheri's educational background, she received her bachelor's degree and first master's in special education from Missouri State University. Later, she pursued administration and got a second master's and a specialist degree from Lindenwood University in educational leadership.

Author website:
https://prayerpawpuppies.wixsite.com/authorsherich apman/books

www.ingramcontent.com/pod-product-compliance
Lightning Source LLC
Chambersburg PA
CBHW060621260626
47161CB00008B/2767